Ten Christmas Shots

BAES OF CHRISTMAS

ELLE WRIGHT

Proofreading:
Paulette Nunlee
5-Star Proofing

Cover Design:
Sherelle Green

Dear Reader

Write a Christmas story, make it funny and light...

That was certainly my intention when I wrote Ten Christmas Shots. Because I LOVE everything about this holiday. The lights. My tree. The gift of family. The cookies. Every. Damn. Thing. Except... Sloane and Maddox had a journey to take and it wasn't always pretty, it wasn't always fun. But it was real.

Revisiting the Wilson family was an emotional process, but I love them so much. If you've read Made to Hold You, you know what I mean. Linc and Layla had their happy ending and are now able to watch their children find love. I love it.

And I LOVE the Cross family. I had so much fun bringing this new family into my world. I can't wait for you to meet them.

Ten Christmas Shots resonated in a way that was personal for me, in so many ways. Essentially, it's a story about finding the magic in life again after devastating heartbreak and loss. I won't go into too much detail here, but I hope you enjoy the ride.

Love,
Elle
www.ellewright.com

Recommended Reading

Ten Christmas Shots features the youngest daughter of the hero and heroine of my novella, MADE TO HOLD YOU, a historical romance that takes place in the 1980s. If you'd like to get acquainted with this family before you read, I recommend starting with that story.

———

Layla Johnson had a picture perfect life: a career as an educator, a beautiful daughter, a son on the way, and a loving husband. Only Layla didn't count on the effect the burgeoning war on drugs would have on her family and her world. And on one rainy night, everything that she worked to attain is destroyed. Now, she's on her own, with two young children, a mounting pile of debt...and the past knocking at her door.

Lincoln Wilson broke the one thing he treasured most. Instead of spending the rest of his life doting on his beautiful wife and children, he's alone, haunted by his many mistakes. Determined to make amends, Lincoln works to put the pieces of his life back together again. And although it's an uphill battle, he is up for the challenge. The last step in Lincoln's program is to prove to his wife that he can be the man she needs. When he shows up on her doorstep ready to reclaim his life, will Layla let him in?

For Mom, I miss you so much. I hope you're smiling.

CHAPTER 1

You're a Mean One, Ms. Grinch

SLOANE

December 15th, This Year

"**W**hat the hell...?" I nearly tripped over an ornament lying in the middle of the floor. "Shit." I set my suitcase down and kicked the gold ball of glass down the hallway. To my right, I noticed the new tabletop Christmas tree near the staircase. "...is this?"

The Christmas music registered next, followed by the sound of giddy laughter and good cheer. Nothing I wanted to be part of today, or any day. My curse-filled rant about following instructions would have to wait, though, because I was expecting something important. I rummaged through my mail and my eyes landed on a blank envelope. Curious, I opened it. It damn sure wasn't the contract I'd expected. I scanned the letter, reading it again just to be sure I'd comprehended it correctly. Actually, it wasn't even a letter. It was more like a memo.

To: Sloane Wilson
From: Hyram Covington Jr.
Re: Us
When I envision my future, I don't see you in it.
I need someone who will cater to me. You're too independent to give a damn.
H
P.S. You're fired.

This punk muthafucka. It wasn't even the breakup that got me. He was right. I didn't give a damn about him or his dick. But that job? Conceptual sketches, custom furniture pieces, textile recommendations, floorplans... I'd worked my ass off for the office space account at the Covington Corporation offices in Downtown Detroit. I should've known better than to mix business with pleasure.

"Sloane?" Courtney peeked her head around the corner. She held up a glass of something alcoholic. "Are you going to join us, or stand in the hallway the entire night?"

I pinched my nose, took in a deep breath, and met my sister's gaze. No sense in wallowing in my misery without liquor, especially at my own party. I snatched the drink from her hand and downed the contents. "I thought I said no Christmas music. I don't want to Fa La La anyone's La right now." *Or ever.*

"It's way past time for you to let this go, sis. It's been years."

"As far as I'm concerned, it hasn't been long enough." It had been years all right. *Years* of tragedy, trauma, bad news, and disappointment. Ten years ago, I married my college sweetheart. My wedding had started with tears instead of joy, and it didn't get better from there. The divorce set me free, though—same date, three years after I'd made the worst mistake of my life. So, I'd vowed to celebrate my freedom, my success, my life without him, every year. Because... *Fuck him*.

"Sloane, come on. It's your party. Don't go back there."

I picked up a snowman figurine. "Look at this shit," I grumbled. "The money spent on this could've been used for Patrón. It's bad enough you decorated the house with—"

"Girl!!!" Courtney laughed and tugged on my arms. "Enough! It's one snowman. Bring your ass in here. We've been waiting for hours. The food is getting cold." She pulled me further into the house.

As expected, my big sister had done an impressive job setting *a* mood. The food looked and smelled delicious, but all I wanted for this ladies' night was less Mariah Carey and more Meg the Stallion. And...

Oh. My. God. There was a tree in my living room. And a Christmas-crazy display of lights and ornaments hanging from the ceiling. And garland spread along the mantle. And one stocking hanging above the fireplace. "Who did this?" I asked incredulously.

I scanned the faces of my guests—my sister and my cousins. They all pointed to the offender without a word.

My cousin Bliss raised her hand proudly. "I did."

Not only was Bliss family, but she was also one of my best friends. Sweet, loyal, giving, kind... We'd grown up together, been there through every triumph, every victory. I found it very hard to be mad at her under any circumstance.

She held up the stocking with my name written in glitter across the top. "Mom did this, though."

My shoulders fell. Now I felt like an asshole. An extremely ungrateful one too. Because I hated everything about this. Yet, there was no way I would ever tell my auntie, my bonus mom, that I hated her creation. But dammit, I needed answers. "Cousin?" I sighed. "Just... I have one small question."

Bliss grinned. "Sure."

"Why?" I thought I'd made myself perfectly clear. My goal every year was to throw a *non*Christmas, *forever*Single party. Period. There was no change of plans, no switch of the theme. I'd planned everything. Food, music, wine. And I'd left my plans in capable hands. Or so I thought.

She shrugged. "It's Christmas."

I blinked.

Someone snorted, another person snickered. I hated all of those heffas, *except* Bliss. Even though she'd Christmas-fied my house. And since there was no use talking to the sweetest person in the room, I turned my attention to Bliss' twin, Blake. "Why did you let her do this?"

Smirking, Blake said, "Because she's Bliss."

Before I could say another word, Courtney shoved another shot glass in my hand. "Damn, Sloane. Drink this, and let's get this party started."

"Can we eat now?" My cousin Dallas asked, rubbing her very pregnant belly. "I'm so hungry."

"Fine," I muttered. "But this conversation is not over."

"We're definitely done talking about this." Courtney walked her bossy ass to the table. "What's done is done."

An hour later, I could care less about the tangent my party had taken, though, because I was full and very tipsy. "I'm stuffed," I groaned, setting my half-eaten dessert on the coffee table.

Dallas snatched a strawberry from my plate. "I have to

hand it to you, Sissy. You certainly know how to throw a party. I'm glad Courtney let you take over." When Courtney glared at her, she shrugged. "What? We all have our strengths, cousin. Love you."

Bliss stood and did a dramatic curtsy. "It's what I do."

I stared at the Christmas tree. Bliss had certainly found a way to accentuate my house décor. And because she knew me, she knew better than to put a bunch of red shit in my house. Rose Gold, Gold, Silver, and even black ornaments made the slim flocked fir tree look full and wide—*and pretty*. But... "I still don't know why you did this." I cleared my throat of the sudden emotion that welled up inside.

Courtney filled my wine glass again. "Because... You've had your mourning period, and we all understand the reasons why."

"Exactly. So why not just give me my little soirée?" I argued. "I'm reframing the day."

"I'm the first person to scream fuck that nigga," Blake said, "and I'm so glad you divorced that sorry-ass, stupid-ass, hoe-ass punk. Good riddance." Her expression softened. "But, I worry that you're embracing the angry part of you so much that you can't see the light at the end of the dark tunnel. You can be happy."

Blake had made an impressive living as The Breakup Expert. Her clients paid her to help them dump their significant others. And now she was talking about light in the dark and telling me I could be happy? Of course she was. Because she'd gone and fallen for her perfect match. I sipped from my glass, eyeing my cousin. "Dex was right... You're so gone over Lennox."

Blake tossed a pillow at me. "Not so gone that I won't kick your ass off that damn couch."

The room dissolved into much-needed laughter. Growing up with these ladies had made all the difference in my world.

My father had cut off communication with most of his family, but I was blessed he and Aunt Vicki stayed close.

"I got fired from the Covington account today," I admitted.

Bliss frowned. "What? I thought they'd already accepted your proposal."

"Yeah, I fucked that up when I fucked Hyram." I finished my wine and stood, pacing the floor. I glared at the Black Santa near the fireplace, fighting the urge to kick it. My anger was with myself, not Santa. No matter how corny that thing was. "I can't believe I did this to myself. Ruined a bomb job prospect for mediocre dick."

Dallas bit into a pickle. "Straight up? It wasn't even good?"

I'd regretted the three-minute interlude shortly afterward because I never slept where I ate. But Hyram was fine, and we got caught up in the moment. "I've had better," I muttered. "A lot."

"I don't miss those days," Blake murmured.

"Enough." Bliss let out an exaggerated sigh and stood. "We're not going to spend any time talking about bad—or meh sex. This is a party." She stepped over to me and squeezed my shoulders. Shaking me a little, she said, "Your next job *and* your next boo will be better than H. Covington." She nodded. "With his pencil dick," she added under her breath.

I cracked up. So did everyone else, because it was rare that Bliss used the "d" word. Hell, she rarely cursed at all. She was the ultimate cheerleader, though. Always in my corner, no matter what, no matter who, no matter why. When we were younger, she asked for three of everything. One for her, one for Blake, and one for me. Even on her own birthday.

Resting my forehead on Bliss' shoulder, I let her hug me. "I love you so much for that. Thank you."

She smoothed a comforting hand over my back and whispered so only I could hear her, "You're going to be okay."

I wanted to believe her. Truthfully, I hadn't been okay in a long-ass time. Despite all my false bravado, I knew I couldn't continue my current trajectory of work, work, and more work. I loved my job, but something felt off. Swallowing hard, I pulled back. "I'll figure out my life eventually." I held up another full bottle of Merlot. "Good thing we still have wine." Bliss eyed Courtney, who glanced at Blake, who nodded at Dallas. Subtle they were not. "What's going on?"

Dallas pulled out a box and set it on the coffee table. "We got you something."

I picked up the wrapped box and shook it. "What is it?"

"Open it." Blake looked at her watch. "Lennox has an early meeting tomorrow, and I would like to get some tonight."

I hated surprises, and every last one of them heffas knew it. But I ripped the paper off the box and opened it. Inside was a scroll. "What the hell?" They watched me silently as I pulled the string off and unrolled it. The first thing I noticed was the Cinderella Castle printed on the thick cardstock. Dread replaced curiosity as I read the invitation aloud. "A three-night luxury vacation to Disney?" I met their waiting gazes. "This is a joke, right?"

"Before you start," Bliss said, "It was my idea, and for a good cause. Remember that non-profit, Christmas Dreams Do Come True?"

Recently, Bliss and I had discussed donating gifts to deserving kids suffering with illnesses for the holiday. The organization had done wonderful and much-needed work in black communities where children were underserved by other charities. "Yes, I remember."

"This year, they did a Secret Santa Silent Auction. We pooled our money and placed a sizable bid on your behalf."

"And?" I asked, still confused what this all had to do with me.

"We won." Bliss smiled.

"And your ass is going to Disney World," Blake added, standing and grabbing empty plates. "I have to go."

The pieces of the puzzle were starting to click. "So, let me get this straight. You bid on trip to Disney for me?"

"And we won," Bliss repeated.

"This is part of your healing," Courtney chimed in. "You need to get back to the Sloane that believed in magic. In imagination. In fun. Time to revisit the *you* that wished she was a Disney Princess."

That Sloane had been chased away a long time ago and I wasn't sure I wanted her bright side, her high hopes back. "I hate Disney World."

Dallas leaned forward, resting her elbows on her knees. "But you used to love it. Just like you loved romance. Just like you loved Christmas once upon a time."

An unexpected tear fell from my eye, and I hurried to wipe it away with my sleeve. "I hate all of you."

Blake handed me a box of Kleenex. "Please don't cry. I can't ruin my makeup by crying with you. I told you... I have a date with my man's d—"

"Anyway," Bliss interrupted. "I'm sure you do hate us right now. But we love you enough to call you on your shit. Running from your emotions never helps. Trust me."

I pointed at her. "This was not supposed to be a therapy session. We're supposed to eat, drink, and laugh."

Raising her arms in surrender, Bliss nodded. "No therapy. It's an intervention, a reset. Take this vacation, use this time to figure out which Sloane you want to be. 'Cause you're a hot mess, girl."

Dallas handed me an envelope. "The trip details are in

there. We know you're not about that Mickey Mouse life, but you won't have to suffer alone."

I snorted. "Right, because I'm not going."

"Yes, you are," Dallas ordered. "And you're taking a date. Preferably someone you want to fuck."

Courtney smirked. "And actually enjoy it."

After the divorce, I'd made it a point to lead with my brain, not my heart. Which meant I stayed away from men and situations that could end with hurt feelings—mine, of course. I folded my arms over my chest. "I don't date."

Blake snickered. "You will next week. And probably the week after Christmas too."

"Even if I did, I don't have time to find a suitable man to take on a damn vacation before..." I checked the trip itinerary again. "...February." I muttered another curse, pinning each of them with an annoyed glare. "On Valentine's Day? Really?" *I hate that holiday too.*

Blake cracked up, falling back on the cushion. Courtney attempted to cover her smile with her hand, while Dallas didn't even bother to hide hers.

"Don't worry," Bliss assured. "We pick the dates. I *am* a matchmaker."

"But I didn't hire you," I reminded her. "Don't you have *paying* clients to match and a toddler to chase around?"

"She's not working alone," Courtney explained. "I've compiled a list of potentials as well. Between my list, Dallas' organization skills, and Blake's—"

Blake cut in, "My bullshit meter will ensure you don't end up with a scrub."

Courtney shook her head. "Anyway, we got you."

Disney World, Christmas auctions, and a few dates.... The entire thing was crazy as hell. But I didn't hate it anymore. I'd never admit it to them, but a very small, quiet part of me wanted to see what they could come up with. Even if I had no intention of going to Orlando or doing anything serious with their date choices. "What if I don't like the men you pick for me?"

Blake shrugged. "Shit, I don't care. What if you do?"

"What she means is—" Bliss rolled her eyes at her twin "— We just want you to be open to the possibility that this might work. Maybe this could be the start of something different for you. Who knows?"

Once again, Bliss had managed to make me question everything I thought I knew in that moment. Because I found myself wondering if I wanted *different*. This journey had the potential to either destroy or reenforce the barriers I'd erected to protect myself over the years. Clearing my throat, I repeated the question in a different way, "What happens *when* I don't like any of your choices?"

A slow smile spread across Bliss' face, almost like she knew something I didn't know. "I'm not worried. I'm very good at my job."

Something shifted inside me. Perhaps it was the little flicker of hope that surged through me at her words and the realization that they were right. It was way past time to do the hard work, to reflect on my past, to deal with myself and my mistakes, to leave my marriage and my dusty ex-husband behind for good. To stop running. "Fine," I relented. "But I have some conditions of my own."

Blake raised her hands and shouted, "Finally."

"No more than ten men. And I'm only giving them twenty minutes to make an impression."

"Done," Dallas said. "Ex-husband is not on the list, of course. But ex-boyfriends are not off limits, and we'll make sure each date is casual."

The fact that she'd mentioned ex-boyfriends made me think she had someone particular in mind, and I didn't know what to think about that. Especially since I could think of no one from my past that I'd want to revisit. I couldn't even imagine spending extended time with *any* man I'd messed around with. "How about we not even call it a date?" I suggested. "One drink. That's all."

Blake laughed. "A shot?"

I smacked my palm on the table. "Even better. And if you're not successful, *all* of you have to go to Disney with me." A chorus of groans validated my initial reservations about the destination. "Thanks for confirming I'm not the only one who hates the thought of going there."

We spent the next few minutes hammering out the details. By the time the plan was finished, I was sure that they would be joining me in Florida. From the moment I'd stepped into my house that evening, I'd experienced the full gamut of emotions—from sadness to happiness, anger and anxiety, disgust and amusement. Then, there was the fear. Everything about this scared the shit out of me because... *What if it worked*?

CHAPTER 2

An Old-Fashioned Family Christmas

MADDOX

"*Welcome back, muthafucka.*"

The greeting I received from my older brother, Broderick, wasn't entirely unexpected. Especially since he couldn't stand my ass. But it had been at least seven years since I'd seen him. Any bad feelings should have dissipated by now. Right?

I dropped my bag on a barstool. "Good to see you, too, brotha."

"Fuck you." Broderick finished his beer and walked out without another word.

Glancing at my younger brother, I raised a brow. "You didn't tell him I was coming?"

With a shrug, Ryker shook his head. "Nah. I figured the element of surprise would be your best bet."

I let out a heavy sigh. "Whatever," I grumbled. Broderick

and I were never close. Partly because he was a liar and a drunk, but mostly because he was everything that I couldn't stand—entitled, spoiled, and manipulative. And, honestly, I didn't have time for his bullshit. Never had. *Never will*. "Is he still wasting his money on women and liquor?"

"What money? He just borrowed $500 from me last week."

Shaking my head, I said, "I told you to stop giving it to him."

Ryker waved a dismissive hand. "Easy for you to say. If he loses his place, he won't end up in *your* spare room."

I snickered. "Damn right. Anyway," I pulled my brother into a hug, "what's up, man?" I spun around in the front room of The Cross Cigar Bar and Lounge. Dark wood, leather furniture, plenty of seating. It wasn't hard to imagine the joint at full capacity—an after-work crowd, live music, thick cigar smoke. My type of spot. "I've seen the pictures, but they didn't do it justice." I stared at my younger brother, pride coursing through my veins at the man he'd become. Solid. Loyal. Business-minded. Consistent. "You did good, man. I remember taking you to smoke your first cigar. I'm proud of you."

Ryker smirked. "None of it would've happened if it wasn't for my silent partner."

I waved him off. "I told you not to mention it. I'm just glad you asked me to be part of this."

I still recalled the conversation we'd had a little over two years ago. Ryker wanted to bring Black business to Ann Arbor, Michigan and proposed opening a lounge. My brother was a Cigar Aficionado. He'd spent years learning about the industry, studying the art of the leaf and the science of growing tobacco. The idea of bringing that excitement to the community, introducing more black men and women to the pastime of smoking cigars, and eventually developing his own brand was something he'd been passionate about for a long time.

"I appreciate your help." Ryker set a wood humidor on the bar top. "I've been saving these for your visit."

For the first time since I'd arrived, I noticed the holiday-themed décor—a string of lights behind the bar and around the windows, a small Christmas tree near the bar, and... Scratching the back of my neck, I asked. "I'm not sure what I expected when I got here, but this..." I gestured toward the ceiling, where an overwhelming amount of mistletoe hung from the ceiling. "—is not it."

Ryker laughed. "That's Tay's doing."

I raised a brow. "You let our sister decorate the bar?"

He slung a clean towel over his shoulder. "Nah. She's having an event here tonight. A Mistletoe Match?"

"Ah." I leaned against the bar. "What the hell is a mistletoe match?"

"It's a party for single women and men, ready to mingle." My gaze flew toward the door, where Taylar stood, a sneaky grin on her face. "Brother." She ran toward me, jumping into my arms.

Wrapping my arms around her, I squeezed her until she pinched my arm. "Hey, Sister."

She tugged her coat off and smiled up at me. "You're a sight for sore eyes."

"Too bad you're not." I mussed her hair, laughing when she shoved me.

After she fixed her hair, she hugged me again. "I missed you."

Taylar and Ryker had been bright spots in a sometimes fucked-up, sometimes uncomfortable situation. Although I didn't grow up in the same household with them, there was mutual respect, sincere friendship, and genuine love between us. "I missed you too," I whispered.

"Did you see Broderick?" she asked.

I met Ryker's gaze, then glanced back at Taylar. "For a second."

She flashed a sad smile at me. "I wish you two could just talk it out."

Frowning, I said, "What for? I didn't do anything wrong —except merely exist." My experience as Maddox Cross, bastard son of Michigan State Representative Ryan Cross, had been one full of ups and downs, great expectations and unspoken demands. Broderick had resented me from the moment I'd entered their lives. That hadn't changed despite my attempts to build a relationship through the years.

"I know that he asked Dad about you. He was concerned."

That was laughable. I'd been to Michigan many times, but he was always conveniently out of town on business. He didn't even show up for me during the hardest time of my life. "That's hard to believe. But enough about him, how are you?"

She squeezed my hand. "I should be asking you that question."

I closed my eyes. I'd spent the better part of the year running from the truth, and while I expected the subject to come up, I just didn't want to talk about it. "I'm good," I lied. "Hungry."

Ryker folded his arms over his chest. "There are trays of food in the back. I can grab you something to—"

"You better not touch those damn trays," Taylar ordered. "I didn't spend hundreds of dollars to have a single chicken wing or a piece of fruit missing."

I held up my hands. "Okay, okay. I still have half of my Jimmy Johns sandwich in my bag."

I stood, stretching for a minute before I walked over to my bag. The front door swung open, and my father stepped into the bar. He greeted me with a smile before he approached me.

15

We didn't exchange words, he simply embraced me. And I let him.

A moment later, he pulled back, squeezing my shoulder. "Son, it's good to see you."

Swallowing past a hard lump in my throat, I nodded. "You too."

"I'm happy you're staying more than a few days this time," Dad said. "Olivia and I thought it would be a treat to go skiing up north the first week of January."

I eyed him skeptically. "Skiing?" I met the amused gazes of my siblings, then faced my father again. "Are you serious?"

Dad cracked up. "Nah, I'm just kidding."

Several years ago, my father wouldn't have joked around like this with me. My teenage years were marked with huge disagreements, due to my belief that he was an elitist snob who looked down on the working class from his ostentatious mansion. And, yes, I'd said that to him. On the other hand, Dad had often accused me of being too "woke" for my own good with no real idea of what it was like to truly struggle. He believed advanced degrees were essential for wealth. I chose not to attend a traditional four-year university. I resented his conservative mindset and, more times than not, we ended up on opposing sides of any argument.

The strain on our relationship had taken its toll on everyone—until we'd agreed to disagree and love each other regardless of our ideologies. And despite the distance between us and our philosophical differences, my father and I had worked hard to maintain a close relationship.

"We're just happy you're here," Dad added, flashing a sad smile. "I know it's been hard on you, losing your mother."

My chest tightened as a familiar pang of sadness threatened to ruin my evening. I took a reflexive step back, dropping my gaze as tears filled my eyes. It wasn't my first Christmas without my mother, but it was the first time I could feel it. She'd passed away last year, a couple of days before the holiday. I'd been so immersed in receiving guests, comforting my stepfather, and ensuring her wishes were followed that I hadn't been able to fully give in to my own grief—until I did. It wasn't pretty, and I didn't want to go back to that dark place.

Letting out a heavy sigh, I asked Ryker for a bottle of water. I didn't speak again until he brought it back. "Thanks," I murmured.

I focused on the water, unable to look at my family, who were no doubt concerned for me. I couldn't face their sad eyes or hear any more condolences. When I'd agreed to spend the holidays here in Michigan, I wanted something other than despair. I wanted to laugh, to drink, to enjoy life again.

"Son?" My father patted my back. "I—"

I cleared my throat. "It's fine, Dad." Finally, I met his waiting gaze. "Mom lived a beautiful life. She was happy and loved until the very end. That's really all I wanted for her." It was my go-to answer whenever someone brought up the most important woman in my life. Over the past several months, I'd learned the hard way that most people didn't want to know my daily struggle or care to hear my overwhelming doubts about navigating the world without my mother. They just wanted to check off a box, make themselves feel better for checking in on me. I'd unpacked all of that in therapy, though. It had taken months, but I was finally at a place where I wasn't so angry all the damn time. I was ready to live the life she'd always wanted for me.

"I love you, brother," Tay said, her voice thick with unshed tears.

"Love you too." I forced a smile her way. Glancing at my father, I asked, "I hope Olivia is making salmon croquettes for breakfast Christmas morning."

Dad chuckled. "She's making all of your favorites. Hope-

17

fully, you'll relent and spend the night with us on Christmas Eve."

"Maybe," I said. "We'll see."

As cliché as it sounded, I'd sort of had the best of both worlds. Devoted parents, and two very present *bonus* parents. While my mother and father were never an official couple, they'd always respected one another—and me. They'd never forced me to choose between them, even when my mother married again and wanted to move to South Carolina. Dad had never questioned my desire to go with my mother, and he'd never made me feel bad about my decision. He'd simply ensured I visited as often as I wanted.

We spent a few minutes catching up while I finished my water and my sandwich. It felt good to be there, to be surrounded by my family. Dad had planned to surprise Olivia with a trip to Dubai before his campaign for the U.S. House of Representatives kicked off. I listened as Ryker shared his next steps for the business. And I learned Taylar had finally quit her corporate job to pursue her love of event planning full-time. Tonight's event was her inaugural event. The concept was genius, designed to match women and men with their true loves, and hopefully, snag their business for the future wedding.

"You're right on time," Taylar mused. "I can use some extra hands setting up the rest of the décor."

I groaned. "Actually, I should probably check into my Airbnb."

"Yeah, no." Taylar ran to the door and lugged a plastic bin over toward me. Without another word, she pulled out a wreath and shoved it into my chest. "Can you hang this up? Then, I'll need your help with the food table."

Before I could argue, she rushed off and disappeared behind a door on the far end of the room. I glanced over at

Ryker, then at Dad, who both shrugged. "Guess I better get to it," I murmured.

Ryker didn't even bother to hide his grin. "Pretty much."

"I better get going." My father stood. "I have a late meeting at the office."

We agreed to meet for breakfast at his favorite restaurant in the morning, and he left. Over the next hour, I helped my sister finish setting up for the early evening event. Taylar had just ordered me to hang even more mistletoe by the door when her alarm went off.

"Shit," she grumbled, racing to clean up the mess. "It's time to stop."

Ryker and I helped move empty bins to the storage room. Her best friend, who'd arrived a little while ago, made sure the tables were cleared. And Taylar... well, she delegated. Finally, the room was presentable, the hors d'oeuvres were displayed, and that damn Mariah Carey song was playing over the speakers. *I hate that shit.*

Guests started arriving shortly before five o'clock. While Taylar and her friend greeted apprehensive women with smiles, I joined Ryker at the bar. "I wonder if she'd notice if I ate one of those chicken wings," I wondered aloud. When Ryker failed to respond, I followed his line of sight to Akira, Taylar's best friend. Obviously, my brother had a thing for the quirky, yet beautiful woman. He'd been distracted since she'd arrived. "Um... bruh?"

He finally looked at me, a slight frown on his face. "Huh?"

"You might want to just say something to her, before she meets her match under the mistletoe."

Ryker blinked. "What?"

I motioned to Akira, who seemed to be conspiring with Taylar about something on the far side of the room. "You were staring."

Touching his forehead, he cleared his throat. "I was just making sure they had everything they needed."

"Yeah..." I smirked. "Right."

Eventually, Taylar let me eat and I settled into a corner booth so I could chill—away from the activity. I'd already been approached by several women, one of them flat out asked if I was her future bae. Unfazed, I applauded her for being so forward, but then I directed her to Taylar.

Akira approached me a few minutes later. "Are you good over here?"

Smiling, I assured her I was just fine. "Looks like Tay got a good crowd."

She scanned the room, a soft grin on her lips. "I know. I'm so proud of her for pursuing her dreams." Glancing at me, she asked, "A couple of the ladies are checking you out, though. Sure you don't want to join in and find your perfect match?" Some things would never change. Although Akira was obviously grown as hell, she still had that hopeless romantic gleam in her eyes.

"No, thanks." I eyed a beautiful woman, who'd been not-so-subtle with her stares. The thought of letting her ride my dick had crossed my mind a few times, but I wouldn't go there. I wasn't trying to be anyone's forever. Or even someone's for now.

"I don't know," Akira chirped. "So many beautiful, accomplished women in the room. Who knows? Maybe they're looking for a successful entrepreneur-slash-musician who knows how to capture an unforgettable moment without even blinking."

Amused, I leaned back in my seat. "Is this your way of asking me to shoot this event?"

She grinned. "Please? I know Tay would love the images for her website."

Good thing I never traveled without my camera. I'd made

a great living at what I did, after all. I pulled my Canon EOS
5D Mark II from its bag. "I got you."

She clapped. "Thank you!"

A moment later, I was working the room, snapping candid
photos of the guests. I blended into the background so that I
could get the shots I needed. The holiday atmosphere, the
comfortable setting, and the mood of the attendees helped my
creativity.

Fully immersed into the environment, I almost didn't
notice her. Almost. I smelled her before I saw her. Her familiar
scent—sweet with a hint of spice—reminded me of the
Tatiana Vanilla Cigar she'd smoked with me the first time we
met. Missed flights, broken promises, and a happy coincidence
had sealed our fates that night. But instead of drowning our
sorrows alone, I'd submerged myself in her. While our brief
interaction all those years ago had barely scratched the surface,
the taste of her lips, the feel of her breath against my mouth
had left an indelible mark on me.

Before I could stop myself, I snapped a picture of her. And
then another one—this time a profile shot. Still a natural
beauty. Her brown skin and dark eyes seemed to glow in the
dim lighting. She wore light makeup; her lips were bare.
Instead of the long waves she'd rocked the first time I'd seen
her, her hair was straight with a part down the middle. I found
myself tracking her movements through the building as she
greeted a few of the ladies in the bar. *What the hell is she doing
here*? It was a Singles event. The last time I'd seen her, she was
engaged to be married, resigned to the life she'd promised to
her fiancé. *Is she divorced*?

"Sloane Wilson!" Ryker called, grinning at her.

Sloane? We didn't share much of ourselves that night
beyond our bodies, but I was pretty sure she'd given me a
different name. I inched toward the bar, determined to hear

more of the conversation she was currently having with my younger brother.

"I haven't seen you in so long, Ryker," she told my brother. "How the hell are you?"

"Good. What brings you in?"

"Meeting my cousin Bliss here. She's working with Taylar on a matchmaking game or some shit like that."

Ryker gestured toward Taylar, who was chatting with some dude in a five-piece suit. "She's over there making connections."

Sloane peered over at my sister. "I'll talk to her in a minute." She slid onto a barstool and ordered a whiskey sour.

It made sense that *Sloane* knew Ryker and Taylar. During a conversation back then, she'd divulged that she was from the Ann Arbor area. Since my father lived in the neighboring city, Ypsilanti, they'd probably attended the same schools.

Instead of focusing on more photo ops for my sister's new business, I eavesdropped as my brother and *Sloane* talked about someone they both knew and an upcoming all-class party. Essentially, I'd morphed from photographer to stalker, which was never appropriate. Snapping myself out of the trance I'd been in since she'd arrived, I took a picture of some random people near the buffet table. While I formulated my plan of action—because there was no way I'd pass up the opportunity to get to know her again—I switched out my memory card.

The low rasp of her voice drew my attention back to her again. "I'm also meeting someone here," she explained. "I agreed to let my sister and my cousins hook me up."

"I know," Ryker said with a chuckle. "Blake tried to convince me you were the one for me."

"Oh hell nah." She laughed. Loudly. "Oh my God, we would kill each other."

Ryker gave her a fist bump. "Exactly. When I told her I knew you, she dropped the subject."

Sloane giggled. "I'm glad she knows when to let something go."

It was a good thing too. Ryker wouldn't know what to do with her. But I sure as hell did. I considered it a pure gift from my mother in heaven that she'd crossed my path tonight. And since the stars had aligned, I looked forward to exploring the beautiful *Sloane Wilson* again.

CHAPTER 3

A Shot of Mistletoe

SLOANE

Kill me now, I thought as I listened to Tim Johnson's snort-like laugh. Glancing at my watch, I prayed the next ten minutes would fly by so I could walk away. All around me, women were vying for attention from the men in the room. And I was sitting there, with a man, thinking I would've had more fun getting waxed. Which... I typed a reminder to myself to schedule my Brazilian before the holiday.

"Sloane?"

My gaze flashed to Tim, who was watching me expectantly. "Huh?"

"What do you like to do?" he asked. "I feel like I've spent the whole time talking about me."

That's because you won't shut the hell up. "I don't like to do anything," I said. "I'm boring."

Tim grinned. "My sister tells me the same thing."

"*Great*," I muttered. The lie was obvious. Of course, I wasn't boring. And I loved to do a lot of things, anything other than this. I finished my third drink of the night. The idea to do shots with my prospective travel partner was brilliant. Except when I took all the shots and he just sat there looking goofy as fuck.

I should've known there would be no love connection. When he'd arrived earlier, his red turtleneck and blazer were immediate turnoffs. Never mind he was too short, too skinny, and too damn nerdy for me. The fact that he'd color-coordinated his outfit to match the Christmas décor was merely icing on the *It-ain't-happening* cake.

I tapped a finger on the tabletop, counting down the minutes until I was free. Free from the first date from hell. Sighing, I picked up my phone and typed a simple text to the women who'd put me in this situation: *I hate all of you. Get me the fuck out of here.*

As if on cue, Bliss strolled over to us. Leaning down, she whispered, "Eight more minutes, cousin," before walking away again.

At least she was nice about it. When I glanced down to my phone, I read the texts from Courtney, Blake, and Dallas—all sent at the same time.

Courtney: *Stop complaining, sis.*

Dallas: *Sit tight. One of Preston's colleagues will be there soon.*

Blake: *Bitch, you got eight minutes. Deal with it.*

I looked at Tim again and fought the urge to throw up. This fool was picking his teeth—with his finger. *Ugh.* Irritated, I fired off another text: *It's okay. Y'all are going to be wearing Mickey ears and eating overpriced Dole Whip with my ass at this rate.*

I cracked up at the barrage of emojis Blake sent, signaling she would not be going anywhere near Disney. But before I could respond back, Bliss breezed over to us again and snatched my phone out of my hand, leaving me there with Tim without entertainment.

He frowned, pointing at Bliss. "Who is that?"

Shrugging, I forced a smile. "Nobody." I rested my chin on my palm. "So, Tim, what do you do again?"

Tim puffed out his chest. On the surface, he wasn't a bad looking man. Maybe Bliss was right. I couldn't judge a book by its red turtleneck cover. "I'm an accountant." He laughed, showing his big teeth and the piece of chicken stuck between his two front teeth. *And he blew it.*

I stood. "I have to go..." I looked up to find Bliss pointing at her watch. She held up a few fingers, signaling I had three more minutes. I plopped back down in my seat. "Never mind," I grumbled.

"This was fun," Tim said. "Maybe we can go to dinner sometime. Courtney told me you loved sushi. I know a great sushi bar we could go to."

That's right. It was Courtney who introduced me to this guy. He worked with her at the hospital. I made a mental note to fire her from date duty. For the next minute and thirty seconds, I sat there quietly. When Bliss came back and handed me my phone, I took it as my cue to leave. I shot him a small smile. "I have to go. I'm sorry, Tim, but this isn't going to work. I wish you luck, though." I stood again and picked up my purse. "You should stay. Maybe you can find your mistletoe match." I started to walk away, but I delayed my departure to address him. "By the way, you didn't get that chicken out of your teeth. You should probably handle that." Without another word, I left him sitting alone and made a beeline for the bar.

Ryker smirked. "That looked painful."

"It was. I need water," I told him.

He set a tall glass on the bar and filled it with ice water.

Ryker and I graduated from high school the same year. We didn't hang out in the same circles, but we'd taken several advanced placement classes together. He'd always been a good guy, but we would never work. Too bad he wasn't my type, though. Because he was certainly easy on the eyes with his dark skin and intense eyes. But he was just Ryker—more like a second cousin than a boo.

"It's obvious you're not into the set-up. Why are you doing this?" he asked.

"Long story," I murmured. "I don't feel like getting into it. Besides, I have twenty minutes before the next guy arrives."

He frowned confusion etched on his features. "Do I want to even know why you have *another* date tonight?"

"Nope."

Chuckling, he shook his head. "I know when to mind my own business."

"You were always good like that," I agreed.

He glanced over my shoulder. "Maddox, can you watch the bar for me?"

I didn't bother to look and see who the hell Maddox was. I just scrolled down my IG timeline. I needed to laugh at a few Reels before Dallas' pick got there. A few minutes later, I watched a short video of a woman telling her man to "bring that dick here." Laughing, I picked up my glass of water and gulped it down.

"Can I get you anything else?"

My eyes flew to the man who'd asked the question, certain he wouldn't be who I thought he was. Unfortunately—or fortunately—I was wrong. *Oh damn*. I pushed myself back because I forgot I was indeed sitting on a small barstool, and nearly fell on my ass. Good thing I had great reflexes because I gripped the edge of the bar, did a quick twist maneuver, and landed on my feet. My phone wasn't as lucky, though. It crashed to the floor and rolled somewhere behind me. Dropping to my knees, I scrambled to grab it before someone stepped on it.

Bliss was faster, though, and she picked it up. "Get your ass up off this floor, cousin," she murmured. "Someone is probably recording your calamity as we speak."

I stood and smoothed a hand over my hair. "Right." I took a few deep breaths before glancing back over to the bar. Yep, he was still there. Still staring. *Still fly*. Turning away, I struggled to gather my thoughts. "I..."

"How many drinks did you have?" Bliss tilted her head to meet my gaze. "Are you drunk? The date couldn't have been that bad."

I swallowed, torn between telling Bliss everything and taking my secret to the grave. I chose to unburden myself and pulled her toward the Ladies Restroom. Once inside, I blurted out, "He's here."

She arched a questioning brow. "Who?"

"Airport guy."

Bliss blinked. "I don't know who that is."

"I never told you this before, but I had a little fling before I got married."

"You had a *lot* of flings before you got married," she said with a shrug.

"No, I—" I glared at her. "I didn't have a *lot* of flings."

"Focus, Sloane."

"Fine." I paced the small restroom and prayed there was no one in the closed stall. I bent low to check for feet. When I didn't see any, I continued, "Before I married Marv, I hooked up with this guy I met at the airport."

It had been ten years, but it was still the single most impactful encounter I'd ever had with a man. We didn't share much about ourselves that night, but our intense connection had been unforgettable. I'd thought about him many times,

28

wondered where he lived, what he was doing, if he'd continued his photography? Did he have children? *Is he married*?

"Wow," Bliss said after I'd told her an abridged version of the story. "That's deep."

I pointed toward the door. "How is he here?"

She shrugged, pulling her phone out of her purse. "I don't know, but I'm telling."

"No the hell you're not." I snatched it away from her and held it up. Bliss was four inches shorter than me, so I knew she wouldn't try for it. "I need to think here. *You* need to help me."

With a smirk, she said, "I got nothing. I just know I don't want to be stuck in the bathroom for hours while you think about it." She held out her hand. "Can I have my phone back?"

I let out a slow breath and handed her the phone. "You're no help."

Bliss giggled. "I don't think I've ever seen you like this."

With my hand on my hips, I said, "Did you see him?"

Maddox was fine as hell. Tall and lean and hard in all the right places. Smooth skin, sincere eyes. And his locs were styled in a sexy-as-hell ponytail. And those lips... *Damn*. I still remembered the way they felt against mine. Shit, I remembered everything about that night like it had just happened yesterday. Our bodies were in sync. While we didn't exchange a lot of words, it felt like we were destined to be in that place, at the same time. When I walked away from him, I'd hesitated. When it was time to marry Marv, I'd paused at the threshold to the sanctuary. And not just because my ex-husband was a sorry-ass cheater. Instinctively, I'd known that I would never have the passion for my husband that I had with the mystery man. And I didn't. Not even close.

"He is hot," Bliss conceded. "But what are you going to do

about it? Hide in here for the rest of the night?" Her phone buzzed. "Oops. Your second date is here."

Panic welled up inside. "I can't go out there and pretend to date someone while he's here."

Bliss' mouth fell open. "Girl, bye. It's twenty minutes. Do what you did with Tim. Act uninterested, and it'll be over before you know it." She left me standing in the bathroom.

I stared at my reflection in the mirror, took a few deep breaths and walked out of the bathroom. The first thing I noticed was Ryker behind the bar. Not Maddox. I tried to ignore the disappointment I felt in that moment, but I wasn't doing a great job at anything tonight.

"*Maybe I should just make up an excuse and leave*?"

"That wouldn't be any fun."

I yelped, whirling around to find Maddox standing behind me. The half-smirk, half-smile on his lips let me know he was enjoying my torment a little too much. And the fact that he wasn't as hot and bothered by my presence as I was by his pissed me the fuck off. Narrowing my eyes, I said, "What the hell are you doing here?"

"I guess I could ask you the same question. *Courtney*."

My cheeks burned. Because, oh yeah, I'd given him my sister's name. *Yikes*. I scratched the back of my neck. "Okay, I lied. I didn't know you. You could've been a..." I sighed, "a killer. Or you... You could've wanted to stalk me or something."

He chuckled and the sound shot straight to my pussy. "And you still make me laugh."

"The point is I never thought I'd see you again."

His gaze dropped to my mouth. "And now I'm here."

"Inexplicably," I breathed.

"Ryker is my brother," he explained. "I'm here for the holidays."

I thought I recalled Taylar mentioning another brother.

But I'd assumed she was talking about their older brother. Wait... "How old are you?"

"Thirty-three," he replied.

"But, you—"

"My father and Olivia had split up for a little while after Broderick was born. He met my mom during that time. They hooked up, he got back together with his wife, then I showed up."

The pieces started to click together. Made sense we were on the same flight to Detroit. He was probably coming to visit his family, and I was returning home from a work trip. "Do you visit a lot?" I asked.

"Not lately," he admitted. "This year is the first time I'll be in town on Christmas Day."

"Oh, that's nice." And I meant it. Despite my own feelings about the holiday, the best part of the season was time spent with family. I couldn't wait for my brother, LJ, to come home for Christmas. I enjoyed game nights and good food, laughter and making memories. "I'm sure they're glad you're here."

"Are *you* glad I'm here?"

The question caught me off guard. As with everything else that had happened tonight, I didn't recover fast enough to toss back a witty response. "I'm not sure what you want me to say. A lot of time has passed."

"You're at a Singles party. Does that mean you didn't get married?"

"Oh, I got married," I admitted. "Then, I got divorced."

"I hope that's a good thing."

"Definitely good." I giggled. "Leaving him was the best decision."

Maddox brushed my cheek with his thumb. "I thought of you often."

I let out a shaky breath. "Same," I confessed.

"What are we going to do about it?"

Bliss had asked me the same question. I didn't know the answer then either. He inched closer to me, and I took a step backwards—right into the wall. And... *Shit, I can't breathe*. "I have a date," I blurted out.

He caged me in and leaned down, brushing his nose against my cheek. "Sure about that?"

The powerful connection we'd shared so long ago was still there, still too strong to ignore. At that point, all it would've taken was two words—*let's go*—and I would've followed him out of the bar right then. Yet, that simple realization also produced a bunch of red flags that had little to do with him and a lot to do with me. I'd vowed to never let the flutters in my heart make my decisions again. The mere act of looking into his eyes, the feel of his finger brushing my skin, and the heat of his body against mine had sent my heart skipping over a cliff. But I wouldn't follow it over. Warring emotions aside, I would not go out like a sappy, horny bitch.

Ducking under his arms and putting some much-needed distance between us, I said, "I'm very sure. Like I said earlier, I never thought I'd see you again. While it's good to know you're okay, it's probably best we keep it moving." Then, I walked away without looking back.

Twenty minutes later, I was ending my shot date with Louis Holter, architect working with Dallas' boyfriend, Preston Hayes. This time, the conversation had flowed freely. There were no teeth-picking incidents. He'd been a perfect gentleman. Funny, interesting, and engaging. But I couldn't stop sneaking glances at Maddox. Now that I knew he was around, I couldn't look away. I'd noticed him moving around the room, snapping pictures, chatting with his siblings, and charming the dresses off of the female attendees. And I hated it. I hated *them* for smiling at him, for flirting with him. Because I wanted to do all of those things myself, even against my better judgment.

"It was good to finally meet you," Louis said, standing. He walked over to me, pulled out my chair, and waited for me to stand. "Maybe we could catch a movie."

Out of the corner of my eye, I caught Maddox taking a picture of a group of women who'd arrived together. One chick, the one with the long legs and tight-ass dress, handed him her business card. And that muthafucka tucked that shit in his pocket.

"Sloane?"

I blinked, forcing my attention back to my not-too-bad date. "Yes?"

"Are you okay? You seem distracted."

"I'm fine," I lied. "Just tired." *Tired of my own bullshit*.

Taylar walked over to us, a wide grin on her face. "You're under the mistletoe," she chirped, pointing upward.

Instinctively, I met Maddox' waiting gaze across the room. I peered at the ceiling, then at Louis. Then, I stepped out from under the stupid plant. I told myself it was because I hated mistletoe and Hallmark movies and corny traditions that didn't mean anything.

Louis let me off the hook, though, and made up some excuse about having a first kiss in the middle of a Singles party. I shot him a nervous smile. "Thanks," I mumbled.

"I'll walk you to your car," he offered.

"Oh, I'm not leaving right now." I pointed over at Bliss. She'd been watching the scene unfold since I'd emerged from the back with Maddox on my heels. "I'm waiting on my cousin."

"I understand. Talk to you soon, I hope." Louis gave me a sweet hug before he made his way out.

A few seconds later, Bliss came over to me. "You know what I think?"

"If I say I don't care, will you tell me anyway?"

"Yep," she said. "I think Louis was perfect for you.

Successful, handsome, personable. But I also think that fate has a way of making you question everything. Maybe you should talk to him."

"Who?"

"Maddox." She folded her arms over her chest. "Sloane, you two need to have a conversation. And not in the back of the bar. Go somewhere quiet."

I shook my head. "No. I'm not going down that road."

She sighed. "You're so damn stubborn."

I hugged her. "You love me anyway. I better go. I have an early meeting. How long are you staying?"

"I told Taylar I would stay 'til the end. Call me when you get home."

Grabbing my purse, I agreed to send a text when I made it to my house. I walked toward the door, intent on ignoring Maddox. But when he called my name, I stopped. "Yes?" I said.

"Have dinner with me?"

"You're under the mistletoe again," Bliss announced, a sneaky smile on her lips.

Maddox and I peered up at the ceiling. Yet, unlike with Louis, I made no move to step away from him. Instead, my feet were planted to the floor, my palms were sweaty, and my heart was pounding hard.

I shot Maddox a sidelong glance and prayed he would move. Then, he finally did. Except he didn't move *away* from me. He moved *toward* me, pulling me into his arms and brushing his lips over mine. Once, twice, three times, before sucking my bottom lip into his mouth and kissing me like we weren't in a public bar, like we weren't standing in front of his siblings and my cousin, like we'd known each other for years. And I loved every moment of it, every moan, every nip, every lick, every touch. Every. Damn. Thing.

When he pulled away, I slumped against the wall, grateful

it was there or else I would've fallen to the dirty floor. It also helped that his strong hands were holding me up too. I took a few breaths and opened my eyes. I scanned the room quickly, noting Ryker's wide eyes, Taylar's open mouth, and Bliss' satisfied grin. I tugged at my collar, straightened my coat, and glanced at Maddox. "Dinner would be nice." I handed him my business card. "Thanks for not letting me fall. Goodnight." Then, I left.

CHAPTER 4

Taste Like Candy

MADDOX

"Why the hell are you paying twenty-five damn dollars for a candle?" I picked up one of the three-wick candles and smelled it. Cringing at the strong scent of chocolate and cream, I set it back down and picked up another one. This one was a little more subtle. It smelled like apples and spices.

"I have a coupon," Taylar said, taking the candle from me and putting it in her basket. "Besides, these make really good gifts."

"Why not just buy gift cards?"

"Because they're not thoughtful," she said with a shrug. "At least, the receiver knows I put some thought into it."

"Yeah, that's bullshit." I didn't understand that reasoning. When I bought a gift card, I considered many things before purchasing. Did the receiver like to eat out? Would they use a spa gift certificate, or would they rather get free coffee for a week? But somehow gift cards were deemed impersonal. Go figure.

Once Taylar paid for her overpriced bath and body products, we went to the next store. Briarwood Mall had once been a bustling mall. Today, though, many of the stores were closed and shops were empty. I'd spent the afternoon with my sister, listening as she talked my ear off about work, her new build, and her potential soulmates. —As in plural, more than one, because she couldn't choose between the engineer or the chef.

"How about you choose the one who makes you happiest?" I suggested as we entered yet another store.

"Maddox, that's not good advice. They both make me happy in different ways." She tapped her chin. "Maybe I should just have sex with both of them and base my decision on who gives the best orgasm?"

I groaned. "Whoa! We're not talking about your sex life, Tay."

"Why not?" She hunched a shoulder. "I'm a grown-ass woman."

"You're still my *little* sister."

She giggled, waving a dismissive hand. "Whatever. How do you know Sloane?"

Ignoring the question, I stopped at a kiosk and eyed the gift cards. "Think Olivia would prefer Macy's?"

"I'm thinking you two hooked up in the past because that definitely wasn't the type of kiss you'd give a stranger."

I held up two different gift cards. "Pottery Barn or Nordstrom?"

"Have you talked to her?"

The simple answer was no. But I'd called Sloane at least twice since the party. She'd yet to return my call, or even text me back. "Maybe she would enjoy a trip to the day spa?

37

Doesn't your best friend own one? I'd prefer to support a black business."

"Yes, she does," she replied. "You know, several of the women at my party asked about you. That kiss shut everyone down, though. Akira talked about it for the rest of the night. Too bad she's fixated on Broderick. He's such a jerk."

The fact that sweet Akira wanted my asshole brother didn't sit well with me. But if I responded to that, Tay would view that as permission to ask more about *my* love life. "What about Neiman Marcus?"

She let out a frustrated curse. "I hate you. Fine. I'll drop the subject. And I told you... Mom would love a gift from the heart."

"Maybe I don't have a heart anymore," I joked. Except I was only half-kidding. And, unfortunately, I couldn't take the words back once I'd said them.

"Maddox?"

Letting out a heavy sigh, I dropped my head. This trip wasn't supposed to be like this. Grief was a normal process. I'd been through all the phases multiple times over the past year. But breaking down in the mall? That was new for me. Most days, I was good. But, damn, I missed my momma. As much as I loved and appreciated Olivia, I wished I was shopping for my mother too.

Christmas had been *our* holiday. Right about now, I'd be grocery shopping with her, helping her purchase gifts for everyone she loved, and hanging her many ornaments on the tree only for her to move them to a different spot. Life was very different without her, and I didn't know how to feel about that.

I felt Tay next to me, watching me. I didn't look up at her, but I imagined sadness clouding her features, tears swimming in her eyes. "Stop staring at me like that," I ordered.

"I'm worried about you," she said, her voice thick with emotion.

I peered at her then, and just like I thought, her eyes were wet, red. "Please don't cry," I said as I fought back my own tears. "I'm fine."

"I'm sure you tell everyone that, but I'm me. We're us."

"Really, sis," I insisted. "I'm good."

You're not." She hugged me, squeezing me tightly. "I just… I want you to know that I'm here for you, okay? You don't have to feel alone."

My shoulders fell and I dropped my chin on the top of her head. "I know I'm not alone."

We stood like that for a moment, and I savored the comfort she offered so freely. I didn't know how much I needed it in that moment.

Eventually, she cleared her throat and pulled back. "Shit." She shot me a watery smile. "I probably ruined my makeup."

I barked out a laugh. I didn't want to give her the bad news, but she would kill me if I let her walk around the mall looking like a raccoon. "Maybe just a little bit."

Giggling, she shoved me. "Let me run in this bathroom." She jogged toward the restroom area.

The line to see Santa had grown considerably over the past half hour. Some kids cried, some screamed, but most of them were just happy to be able to sit on his lap. I took a seat near the smoothie place and watched as mothers readied their children for their photo op. One of my first paying photography jobs was snapping the pics of children at the local mall near my house. I made good money in tips that year, and it had cemented my desire to pursue my passion.

Pulling out my phone, I snapped a pic of Santa talking to one of the Elves. Looked like the old man was trying to holla. But the pretty elf seemed to have eyes for the photographer. Catching moments like these was one of my favorite perks of the job. I'd heard and seen everything, from breakups to hookups, and all the shit in between. I'd seen brides elated and grooms flirting with bridesmaids. I'd captured moments of devastation and moments of bliss.

Speaking of Bliss... I spotted the woman standing in the long line bouncing a toddler in her arms. She was looking my way too. Standing next to her were three women and a man, and all of them were looking at me as well. Unlike the other night, I couldn't avoid her, so I stood and headed over to her group.

On the way, I scanned the area, wondering if Sloane was nearby. She wasn't. It had been two days since we'd kissed, and I could still taste her. So much that I'd spent a stupid amount of time trying to figure out what type of candy she'd been eating that night. I'd settled on SweetTarts.

As I neared them, I overheard the tail end of their conversation. "... because Sloane is trippin' if she's going to let Mr. Fine-ass—"

"Hey," Bliss cut off the woman who I now knew was her twin. "It's good to see you." She introduced me to her sisters, her brother, and her mother. "This is Maddox."

I shook their hands. "Good to meet you."

"Blake is dating Lennox, Ryker's friend," Bliss said.

"Oh, okay." I'd known Lennox for years. We'd hung out quite a few times when they were attending Howard University. "Tell him I said what's up."

"And this is Naija, my baby girl," Bliss explained. "We're visiting Santa for the first time."

I smiled at the baby and held out my hand. "Hi, Naija." The little beauty laughed when I made a silly face at her.

Bliss' mother beamed. "You have a way with kids, Maddox."

"He's a photographer, Mom," Bliss said. "I should've had you snap the pics."

"Anytime," I offered. "I'll be in town for a few weeks if you want me to shoot your family."

Her mother asked if I could take pictures at their home after Christmas, and I agreed to set aside some time. We exchanged business cards while Bliss' twin and her brother started arguing about color schemes.

Blake smacked her brother in the shoulder. "Duke, we're not wearing black for a Christmas photo shoot. And stop eating my pretzels."

Chuckling, I said, "I'll be in touch after the holiday."

Bliss handed her mother the baby. "Got a second?" she asked me. I eyed the curious gazes of her family and nodded, gesturing toward a row of chairs. She walked ahead of me, just far enough to be out of earshot from her family. "I probably shouldn't do this, but Sloane is in the mall."

I nodded, unsure how I should respond. Or *if* I should respond.

"She's at the wine tasting kiosk waiting for her date," she continued.

At the event, she'd been with two different men. Curious, I asked, "Another date? At the mall?"

Bliss laughed. "It's convenient."

Still unsure how to respond, I just stared at her and tried not to let the fact that Sloane was on yet another date—with someone other than me—frustrate the hell out of me. "Well, tell her I said hi." I saw Taylar walk out of the bathroom and into a small boutique. "I should probably go."

"I'm sure you're wondering why I told you this, right?"

"The thought did cross my mind," I said.

Bliss shifted from one foot to another. "I think you should go talk to her."

"Why?"

She sighed. "Can I be honest?"

"Of course."

"You know you messed up, right?"

I folded my arms over my chest. "How so?"

"You kissed her, and then you let her leave when you should've walked her to her car."

I blinked.

"Now that she's had some distance, some time to process everything, she's not going to answer your call. Even if she wants to."

I closed my eyes and took a deep breath. "So my question to you is why should I bother then?"

"Because I know my cousin. Trust me. She wants to answer the call, but you have to make her see that it's safe to do so. I have to go. The wine kiosk is near Macy's. Good luck." She patted my arm and started walking back to her group.

"Wait?" I called after her.

She turned to face me. "Yes?"

"Why are you doing this?"

"It's what I do." She waved at me and rejoined her group.

And I sent a text to Taylar letting her know I had to handle something and took my ass over to the wine tasting kiosk.

Sloane was seated at a table, looking down at her phone. But no date. I took that as a sign and approached her, sliding into the seat across from her. "I'm still waiting on dinner." She glanced up at me, eyes wide. "Since you said it would be nice."

Her mouth fell open. "Uh..."

I reached out, placed my hand under her chin and gently closed her mouth. "You wouldn't be so surprised to see me if you'd actually answered one of my calls."

Sloane cleared her throat. "I..." She grumbled a curse. "Okay, I suck."

I chuckled, grateful for her candor. "Glad to know you feel the same way I do."

The corners of her mouth quirked up. Then, she laughed. "So you're agreeing that I suck?"

I threw my hands up in the air. "You said it first."

"I'm sorry," she said. "I probably should've at least texted you back."

"What would you have said?" I challenged.

Shrugging, she admitted, "That I can't go to dinner with you."

Damn. "That's... honest."

"I know no other way to be." Sloane sipped from her glass of wine. "When we met, the best part about the encounter was that we didn't know each other. Because of that, you've always been this... I don't know. You've always been this dream, my escape. It was perfect, exactly what I needed. I'm hesitant to ruin that with reality." She bit down on her bottom lip. "Does that make sense?"

Definitely. I understood where she was coming from because I felt the same way. At the time, I was between jobs and relationships. I was at a crossroads, searching for direction. I found it that night. The experience had inspired my best-selling collection. I'd left her invigorated and determined to make my mark. The next day I'd landed a job at a top hip hop magazine, and I'd been soaring ever since.

"Maddox?" she whispered. "If I have dinner with you, it wouldn't be *just* dinner."

Sloane was right, and that simple truth made everything complicated. Dinner was a formality, a pre-cursor to my mouth on her clit and my dick in her pussy. Dinner was a promise to explore the connection that had been seared on my mind. Dinner was the realization that I couldn't walk away from her again without feeling like I'd lost something important. And I didn't want to lose anything or anyone else.

"How about lunch then?" I asked

Her eyes flickered with amusement, and she tossed me a

lopsided grin. "How about a drink?" She glanced at her watch. "Apparently, I just got stood up and I'm free for twenty minutes."

Several minutes later, we were on our second tasting. This time, she tried a Merlot while I sampled a Syrah. We'd kept the conversation polite, not too intrusive, not too personal. Sloane's face lit up when she'd shared a little about her business, Sloane Interiors. She'd just landed a new account and couldn't wait to get started on the design.

While she talked, I found myself transfixed by her. Today, she wore dark jeans, a t-shirt and Crocs. Her hair was pulled back into a ponytail, and she smelled like fruit and flowers. Grapefruit and pear, daisies and jasmine.

"I'm happy to see you're still pursuing your passion. Your work is amazing."

I recalled briefly discussing my career with her back then— the pitfalls of the industry, the disappointments, the inconsistent income. At that time, so much of my life was in flux that I'd contemplated quitting. The fact that she remembered the conversation kind of confirmed that I'd made the right decision coming to the wine kiosk. Raising a brow, I asked, "You looked me up?"

Her eyes locked on mine. "I did."

"I'm glad."

A slow smile formed on her full lips. She pointed at me. "Don't let it go to your head, though."

"I'll try." Leaning closer, I said, "I'm curious about something."

She arched a brow. "What is that?"

"Why were you meeting a date in the mall?"

Her tongue darted out to moisten her lips and I followed the movement like a hawk. "It's this thing. My sister and my cousins have set me up on ten short dates, so that I can find someone to accompany me on a trip to Disney World."

Okay, so I wasn't expecting that. But now I was even more intrigued. "You're going to Florida?"

"In February. The trip was a gift from them. They told me I needed to find some magic because apparently I'm too jaded."

"You don't believe in magic?"

She shrugged. "I used to," she admitted. "Now, not so much."

Bliss' words replayed in my mind. *Make her see that it's safe*. "I know the feeling," I confessed. "My mother died last year. Christmas was always important to her, and it just doesn't feel right celebrating it without her. Ya know?"

Her expression softened. "I'm so sorry. I can't imagine what you're going through."

"I tell myself every day that living is what she wanted most, so I should do my best to live a full life. But on days like today, I really just want to give her a hug or hear her voice."

"You're also human, and you are allowed to feel how you feel. Honestly, I don't know what I would do without my mom."

"Are you close to her?"

She smiled. "Very. When I think of a strong woman, I think of her. The things she's been through... Many would've given up. But she persevered. Now, she's retired and living her best life with my dad."

"That's nice."

"What about your father?"

"We're good. I'm actually looking forward to spending more time with him and my siblings."

"Where do you live?"

I eyed her. A week ago, I would've told her I lived in Charleston. My stepfather had moved to Los Angeles to be near his family. And there was no reason to stay there anymore. I'd considered moving to Atlanta or New York. But

45

everything was in limbo right now. Still, I told her, "South Carolina."

Her face lit up. "I love the Carolinas. We travel to the Outer Banks every year for Thanksgiving."

"Really?"

"Yep. Maybe I'll run into you next time I visit."

I couldn't resist, so I asked, "Will you have dinner with me then?"

She laughed. "You're too much." She stood. "I should probably go, though. Your twenty minutes are up."

I leaned back in my chair. "Should I count it as a win that you gave me forty minutes?"

"Absolutely." She placed her hand on top of mine. "I had a good time today. Thanks for the wine." She started to walk away but stopped. Turning to me, she said. "If I say yes to dinner today, I'd probably cancel tomorrow."

I grabbed a business card and set it in her palm. "I'm going to leave the ball in your court, then. Call me when you're ready to accept the invitation."

Her gaze fell to my lips, and I wanted to lean in and kiss her. But I waited. If this was going anywhere past the wine kiosk, she would have to make the move. "I'll think about it." She brushed her mouth over mine. "That's for knocking me off my square the other night."

I gripped her wrist. "Feel free to return the favor anytime."

She smirked. "I'll think about it," she repeated. "Bye, Maddox."

Sloane disappeared into Macy's a few minutes later, and I knew one thing for certain. While we'd only spent a short time together, it was clear that wine tasting would never be enough for me. I wanted more.

CHAPTER 5

Negroni, Please

SLOANE

I'm so over it.

My day had started with a Sausage McMuffin and a shot of Hi-C orange with date-number-five, who'd chosen McDonald's because he was a recovering addict and liked to stay away from bars. Unfortunately, I'd caught the guy watching porn on his phone when I'd returned from the restroom. I'd hightailed it out of the restaurant and promptly sent a text to Blake to let her know that Lennox could no longer participate in any matchmaking duties. Full stop.

By the time I made it to Starbucks, I was convinced their little Hook Sloane Up Plan was doomed. And I couldn't understand why I felt happy *and* disappointed. While standing in line, I checked my email, pleased when I received a thumbs up for my latest design. I responded with a request for an in-person meeting to go over timelines.

Christmas music played on the overhead speaker, and I found myself swaying to the tune. It wasn't the first time I'd felt all warm and fuzzy and merry this week either. At my parents, I'd helped my nephew decorate a gingerbread house. Yesterday, I sang along to Boyz II Men's "Let It Snow" at my office. I even agreed to go to Holiday Nights in Greenfield Village with my family. My first visit to the museum had been quite the experience. We'd spent hours exploring, visiting the historic districts, enjoying the rides. I'd even put on skates and snapped a selfie before I wiped out on the ice.

After I placed my order, I took a seat at a booth near the door. Date-number-six should arrive in the next half an hour. Until then, I decided to work. I'd just put the finishing touches on another floor plan when I heard a familiar voice call my name.

"Sloane?"

I rolled my eyes. The last person I expected or even wanted to see was Hyram Covington. But there he was, standing in front of me. "What the hell do you want?" I asked.

Hyram sighed. "Your assistant told me I could find you here."

It had been five days since he'd fired me via memo, and I was still salty about it. "What do you want?" I repeated.

He slid into the seat across from me. "We need to talk."

I sipped my peppermint mocha and waited. When he didn't say anything, I did. "Well? You said we needed to talk. Say something."

He cleared his throat. "This isn't easy for me, but I wanted to apologize to you."

I leaned back in my chair, crossing my legs at the knee. "What for?"

"I was angry." His gaze darted from me to the table to my breasts to the wall, then back to me. "Hurt, really. I was wrong for lashing out at you. What happened between us should never affect work."

I studied him. It was no secret that Hyram wielded power in the Covington Corporation because his father owned the company. People talked and he had a reputation for being a fuck-up, plain and simple. The only thing he had going for him was his name. And he was hot. But that's it. I hadn't spent much time with him, but it was clear to me that he was more cocky than sincere. The little display he'd put on, the attempt to show regret, his tone of voice told me he'd done this out of necessity, not because he truly wanted to make things right.

"Your father sent you?" I asked.

He crossed his hands on the table. "He suggested I contact you, yes."

"Thanks for the apology, but you can kiss my ass."

"The company would like to offer you the agreed-upon contract. We're willing to up your fee by ten percent, for your inconvenience."

My father once told me that all money wasn't good money. I'd learned that lesson time and again through the years—in my marriage and at work. My ex-husband offered to pay alimony if I allowed him to slip in my bed every once in a while. Inappropriate touches, uncomfortable stares, and even veiled threats had colored my corporate work experience. And when I left my husband, I'd quit my job to start my own company.

I contemplated the offer for a few more minutes. The reasons to take the job outweighed my petty need to tell Hyram to go fuck himself. Still, I couldn't bring myself to accept. "I don't think so, Hyram."

He frowned, scratching his jaw. "What? You're turning me down?"

"Exactly."

"Not even for fifteen percent above the proposed amount?"

As tempting as it was, I couldn't do it. "No. You've already proven that you're an entitled prick. I won't work with someone who throws temper tantrums when they can't get their way. I will not let anyone treat me the way you did and get away with it. Period. And don't worry about telling your father what I said because I'll tell him myself. It's better he hears it from me because I don't trust you to do the right thing."

He snickered. "Wow. You're walking away from money and connections because I dumped you?"

"You know I don't give a damn about you. That's why you 'dumped' me," I threw up the quote sign because I would never classify what we had as something that had to be dumped, "right? So take that shit somewhere else."

Hyram's jaw ticked as annoyance washed over his face. But he knew better than to continue this conversation in the middle of Starbucks. He nearly tipped the chair over in his haste to stand. "I hope you don't regret this, Sloane."

Even if I did, I'd never tell him. "I won't. Have a good day."

A few minutes after he left, I packed up my laptop and glanced at my watch. Date-number-six was late, and he was about to get canceled. I fired off a text to the ladies: *Another no-show. Bliss, you're fired too.*

Bliss responded right away: *He's coming. No worries.*

I felt someone brush past me to sit at the booth next to me. I didn't bother to look up, though, because I was too busy laughing at Blake's text: *Is it just me or did anyone else think Sloane would've at least seen someone's dick by now? Let's get this show on the road. Now.*

The man next to me cleared his throat and I glanced at him quickly before turning my attention back to my phone. Wait... I looked at the man again. "You?"

Maddox flashed a dimpled grin. "Hey."

"How are you here? I mean, why are you here?" I asked him incredulously.

He shrugged. "Grabbing a coffee. It is a public place, right?"

"Did you know I would be here?" I pressed.

"How would I know that?" He tossed back.

He has a point. I shifted in my seat. "This is too weird."

Maddox sipped from his cup. "Not that weird. People run into people all the time at the coffee shop."

That's also true. Yesterday, I ran into Ryker at the gas station, so it wasn't out of the realm of possibility that this was simply a coincidence. "Fine, but I have a date."

"What number is this?" he asked.

"Six," I replied.

"And here I am still waiting on one."

A smile tugged at my lips. "I told you I'd think about it." I'd spent valuable time obsessing over it, actually. The short time we'd spent together at the mall had only made me want more time with him. But I was holding firm on my promise to myself. I already thought about him entirely too much to be trusted on a date with him. I knew myself and I'd probably hop on his dick before the salad arrived.

"Are you thinking about it now?" He shot me a knowing glance. "Because I'm ready when you are."

I opened my mouth to answer him, but nothing came out. My resolve was weakening under his intense stare. And he smelled too damn good.

"Sloane?"

I glanced up at ... "Richard?"

"Hey, you." My fifth-grade boyfriend slid into the chair across from me. "I'm sorry I'm late."

Speechless, I shot Maddox a sidelong glance before meeting Richard's gaze again. "I didn't realize you were my date," I admitted. "I haven't seen you since—"

"You stood me up for prom?"

"Oh yeah. That." I finished my coffee. "Sorry."

"It's no problem. Can I get you a refill?"

"Sure." I gave him my order and waited for him to leave before I addressed Maddox again. "If you're going to sit there, don't look at me like that."

"I promise I'll be good," he said. "Has the time already started ticking?"

"I'm not answering that."

He laughed. "I take that as a yes."

"Shut up."

Fourteen minutes and one shot of expresso later, I was ready for this date to end. "I didn't know you needed a license to be a funeral director," I said. "That's interesting."

"It's a very rewarding career," Richard explained.

"I bet," Maddox grumbled.

I'd failed at acting unaffected by Maddox' presence. He was driving me crazy. At one point, his thigh brushed against mine and I almost toppled off the bench. I told myself it was because I was trying to get away from him, but I knew it was really because I wanted to sit on his lap—or his face. *Or both.*

Richard seemed oblivious to my inner turmoil though. He'd talked ad nauseam about funerals and the embalming process. And the entire time, I was thinking about Maddox. Maddox' hands. Maddox' lips. Maddox' dick. At one point, I was concerned that all the funeral talk was bringing up bad memories for Maddox since he'd shared that he recently lost his mother. But it appeared he was just fine with the conversation because I'd caught him snickering quite a few times. More than likely at my expense.

My phone buzzed on the table. I glanced at the screen.

Maddox: *He's not the one for you.*

I cracked a smile, and sent a quick response: *Really? What gave it away?*

The tiny dots bounced around and his reply came a few seconds later: *The drool on your chin from your little catnap a few minutes ago.*

My cheeks burned and I prayed he was just playing with me. Just to be sure, I wiped my face with a napkin before I typed: *I didn't fall asleep.*

Maddox: *You absolutely did. Right around the time he started talking about cremation.*

I giggled. *Shut up. You promised to be good.*

Maddox: *I'll be good when you admit that you want me.*

Dammit, I did want him. I set my phone face down on the table and forced my attention back to Richard. "Well, it was good to see you again." I stood and tucked my planner into my bag. "I have a meeting across town, so I should probably get on the road."

Richard hugged me. "Oh yeah. Maybe we can do this again?"

That would be a hell no. But since he was my first-grade teacher's son, I decided to be nice. "We'll see. Tell your mom I said hello."

"I'll walk you to your car," he offered.

I eyed Maddox who was now staring at me unabashedly. "I'm fine," I assured. "Have a great day."

Richard squeezed my shoulder. "You too."

The moment Richard left the café, I glared at Maddox. "You're killing me."

He barked out a laugh. *Shit, even his laugh is sexy.* "I just want you to be honest with yourself."

I picked up my bag. "I am honest. Honestly leaving your ass here. Bye, Maddox."

"When are you going to stop getting gutter balls, sis?" My brother, LJ, shook his head and he wiped his bowling ball off with a rag. "We're losing to Mom and Dad."

Our first game was not even close. And this game? Yeah, pretty much the same. But being with my siblings, eating pizza and drinking Dr. Pepper, playing one of our favorite games... *Priceless.*

I glared at him. "Shut up, punk. Mom and Dad have bowled on a league since before we were born. They have a competitive advantage."

"Excuses. That's all I hear." He held his ball low at arm's length, scooted to the right an inch, aimed his ball, then threw his patented hook ball. Because my brother could've been a professional himself. *Strike.* LJ popped his collar and strutted to the bench, kissing his pregnant wife and giving Courtney a high-five. Glancing at me, he said, "That's how you put a score on the board."

I rolled my eyes. "Shut up. Get on the Tonk table, and I'll show you how to win something." Earlier in the day, we'd played cards with my parents and, let's just say, I won enough money to buy the Nike running shoes I'd been wanting. "I'm willing to take your money again. I need a new workout outfit."

He shoved me playfully. "Oh, I let you win. Now I don't have to buy your ass a Christmas present."

I laughed, and it felt so good. My brother and his growing family had moved to the DMV area months ago and I'd missed his face. I glanced over at my parents, who were huddled together on the couch, giggling like they were newlyweds and not getting ready to celebrate forty years of marriage next year. The example they'd set for us had been invaluable. My father was proof that redemption was possible, that a person could rise from the ashes and thrive. And my mother had taught us the importance of forgiveness. Dad's addiction could have destroyed them, but they'd overcome the adversity and were happier than ever. Good thing, because I wouldn't be here if they weren't able to make it work.

I walked over to my parents and squeezed in between them. My mom giggled. "Babe, what are you doing?" She patted my thigh. "Shouldn't you be preparing to throw your next gutter ball?"

"Oh!" I said. "You got jokes too, Mommie?" How are you gone do me like that?"

Dad chuckled. "Girly-girl, I don't understand how you've been bowling your entire life and can't even knock down eight pins."

I rested my head on my father's shoulder and watched Courtney pick up a spare. "I just think the awesome bowler gene skipped me."

"You just need to practice. After the holiday, we'll come back. Just me and you."

I kissed his cheek. "Thank you." My watch buzzed and I glanced at it. My seventh date should be arriving momentarily. According to Courtney, he was her colleague's brother and a pilot, which was kind of intriguing. This time, she'd sent a pic and I approved. Still, I couldn't help but wish it would be Maddox. Yesterday at the coffee shop, I realized I liked being around him, even when we were just sitting next to each other, even if he was teasing me. He made me laugh. And, damn, he made me horny. His mere presence sent my body into overdrive. *So why can't I accept his invitation*?

"What's wrong, babe?" My mother asked, brushing a hair from my forehead. "Are you okay?"

"I'm fine," I lied. "Just thinking."

"About your date?"

My eyes widened and I glanced at my mother. "You know about the date?"

"We know about all ten of the dates?" Dad replied.

I bit down on my bottom lip, curious what they thought of this experiment. "Any advice?"

Dad chuckled. There was something about my father's laugh that made me feel safe, secure. Growing up, we'd spent a lot of time doing fun things—impromptu trips to the amusement park, drive-in movies with buttery popcorn, swimming lessons. Sometimes we'd just sit on the patio drinking his favorite pop, Dr. Pepper. When he'd shared his story with me years ago, I couldn't imagine him as an addict because he'd always been so strong, so confident, so dependable. But he'd been very candid about his shortcomings, and because he'd always been truthful with me, I'd vowed to return the favor.

My mother stood. "My turn. A kiss for good luck?" She winked at my dad.

Dad pulled her down on his lap and kissed her. "You don't need it, LaLa. You're actually good, unlike someone we both know and love."

"Hey!" I nudged him with my shoulder.

They kissed again and my mother stood and went to take her turn. My father wrapped his arm around my shoulder. "Want to know what I think, Girly-girl?"

I peered up at him and nodded. "Of course."

"I think you have to let go of your pain before you can find your forever."

The tears welled up in my eyes fast, and before I could stop them, they fell. "Oh damn," I cursed.

He dabbed my cheeks with a handkerchief. "It's okay to cry. You've spent a lot of time holding it in."

"Why did...?" My voice cracked. "How do I do that?"

"Open your heart, purpose to forgive—him and yourself. You'll be surprised how good it feels to be free of that burden."

I squeezed my eyes shut and more tears spilled onto my cheeks. "I knew he wasn't right, Dad. Everyone told me not to marry him. And I thought I knew best. How can I trust that I won't make the same mistake again? How do I know I won't fall for some man's bullshit all in the name of love?"

"You won't," he said. "And it's okay. Baby girl, your experience shapes your future. Without the hurt, without the disappointment, you wouldn't be Sloane Wilson of Sloane Interiors. You wouldn't have worked so hard to get where you are. I'm proud of you. I'm proud of the woman you are. You should be, too, because you're amazing."

I groaned. "See what you did." I wiped my eyes. "Why are you like this?"

He barked out a laugh. "Time, Sloane. I wasn't always this introspective. I hurt your mother so much. But what I came to realize? The true test for me was being able to forgive myself for hurting her. Once I'd done that, I was able to love her the way she deserves to be loved. You'll get it eventually. I will tell you this, though... You won't figure it out in twenty minutes —and a shot."

I sucked in a deep breath and stood. Dad had given me great advice, and I loved him for it. I kissed his brow. "Thanks, Daddy. I should probably fix my makeup before my date."

"I say you cancel the date and work on your game."

I giggled. "Not a chance. Right now, it's more about the principle than the actual date."

He shook his head. "Whatever you say."

I squeezed his shoulder and made my way toward the restrooms, replaying the conversation in my mind over and over. A huge part of me knew this date would be a bust too. I didn't want to meet the pilot. I didn't want to have a shot with anyone else. I wanted to have *dinner* with Maddox.

I did a quick touch-up in the restroom mirror, fixed my clothes, and headed toward the bar intent on getting this date over so that I could text Maddox. But when I rounded the corner, I stopped in my tracks because not only was the pilot sitting at the bar, so was Maddox. *Perfect, albeit peculiar, timing.*

CHAPTER 6

Naughty or Spice

SLOANE

True to form, my genuine glee at spotting Maddox near the bar had morphed into uncertainty with a heavy dose of dread and topped off with more than a pinch of desire. It was hard to keep my eyes off him because he looked damn good in black jeans, boots, and a fitted sweater. *So. Damn. Good.*

Next to him, the pilot looked like someone's sorta attractive uncle. *Poor tink.* "Thanks for meeting me here at the bowling alley, Carl."

"I hope I'm not too early. Can I order you a drink?" he asked.

I noticed the slow smile that spread over Maddox's face and wondered what he was thinking. Forcing my attention back to Carl, I shrugged. "I'm not drinking today. But you can buy me a Dr. Pepper."

"I can do that." Carl waved the bartender over and placed

our order—a Dr. Pepper for me and a beer for him. "Courtney has told me a lot about you."

I didn't know that. "Really? What did she say?"

"She told me you were beautiful, accomplished, funny."

I grinned. "I am all of those things." When he chuckled, I laughed too. "If I'm honest, though, she didn't tell me anything about you."

Carl gave me the quick version of his life—where he lived, where he worked, what he liked to do when he wasn't in the air. "I'm divorced, one child."

Sipping my soda, I nodded. "How old is your baby?"

"He's fifteen. My ex-wife and I married young and divorced early."

I hummed. "I can speak to that too."

"See, we already have a couple of things in common. What about you?"

"I live in Ypsi, work for myself and I like to eat." I cracked up at myself. "Just kidding. Of course, I love to eat. But I also like to run and swim."

"Ah, did you swim competitively?"

"I did. Only black girl on the swim team. I won the state championship for my high school too."

He gave me a slow clap. Normally, something like that would've come off corny, but I liked it. "That's even better."

We chatted for the next ten minutes about a little bit of everything—from books to food to snow. Surprisingly, I felt comfortable with Carl. Not as comfortable as I felt with Maddox, but still... "I should probably get back to the game," I said. "I'm bowling with my family." Carl stood and reached out to help me to my feet. "Thanks."

"Can I see you again?" he asked.

I glanced over at Maddox, then back at Carl. Then, back at Maddox. The pilot was definitely a winner. His low voice would've made me drop my panties—about six days ago. I knew we'd have a good time together, but... "No."

He blinked.

So did I because I'd just shocked the hell out of myself. "Um, I didn't mean it like that."

He flashed a soft, dejected smile. "In the short time I've been here, I get the feeling you don't say things you don't mean, Sloane Wilson."

My shoulders fell. "I'm sorry, Carl."

"It's okay." He squeezed my hand. "It was good to meet you."

I nodded. "Merry Christmas."

After Carl left, I eyed Maddox again. Tilting my head, I observed him, studied his profile. The Pistons were down twenty points and he seemed focused on the game. During my date, I'd overheard him talking to the bartender about the team's losing season. Even then, I'd wanted to join in the conversation just to hear him talk, to hear his thoughts about basketball—or anything.

Sighing, I walked over to him and hopped onto the barstool next to him. "I've been thinking."

He took a long pull from his beer bottle. Without looking at me, he asked, "About?"

"You."

Maddox shot me a sideways glance. "What about me?"

"And... dinner." I glanced back at my family and noticed Courtney watching us with interest. I couldn't be sure, but it looked like she was smirking. She was definitely texting some-one. And then she... *Did this heffa just snap a pic of us*?

He dropped his head and tapped a finger against the bar. "I'm not really a stalker."

I laughed. "Do you feel like one?"

"I'll admit that I've been completely focused on you and this..." He placed his hand on top of mine, stroking my thumb with his. "Whatever *this* is between us. Real talk, I haven't felt normal in a long time. And the simple act of sitting next to you makes me feel like I'll make it out of this holiday hell intact."

A moment later I was still staring at our hands and how right they looked together. He'd articulated everything I'd already been thinking. His words settled something in me, confirmed what I'd been fighting hard to ignore. I didn't want to get into how he knew I'd be at the bowling alley, but I suspected he had some help from my little matchmakers.

"Honestly, I'm glad you're here," I confessed. "Maddox, I can't promise that I'll want to talk to you tomorrow, but in this moment, I want to have dinner with you."

He smirked. "Tonight?"

"I'm hungry." *In more ways than one.* I stood and held out my hand. "Before we leave, though, I promised my family one last game. Want to join us?"

Slipping his hand in mine, he stood. "Lead the way."

Eight frames of more gutter balls later, I'd finally hit seven pins on my first try. I jumped up, fists in the air. "Yay!" I gave Maddox a high-five.

He grinned. "Good job."

"Thanks. I might score more than fifty this game."

"Finally, Girly-girl!" my father shouted.

LJ rolled his eyes. "It would've been better if you'd got a, oh I don't... A strike?"

I glared at him. "Don't hate." I picked up the ball again. Maddox might be good for my bowling game. After all, I couldn't let him see me flounder too much. I aimed the ball, took a deep breath, and rolled it down the lane. I made a dramatic motion with my hands, almost willing the ball away from the gutter. Behind me, I heard the claps and felt the eyes on me. But that damn ball hated me because, right at the last minute, it curved and missed the pins.

"Aw," Courtney said, approaching the ball return. "That's unfortunate, sis." She smacked my shoulder. "At least you tried your best."

I muttered a curse. "Shut up."

She leaned closer. "Cheer up," she whispered. "You got Ho Ho Hottie over there ready to kiss it and make it better."

I cracked up, shoving her away from me. "You get on my damn nerves."

I took a seat next to Maddox. He held up a hand and I smacked his palm. "Good try," he told me. "But you should really practice more."

Nudging him with my shoulder, I said, "Says the man who has a two-twenty going into the ninth frame."

"I bowled on a league for years," he explained. "Maybe I'll sign up again next year."

"How fun," I muttered, sarcasm dripping from my tone.

Maddox took his turn and, once again, bowled a strike. *Show off.*

My father walked over to me. "Now this guy I like."

I peered up at my dad. "Really? Because he can bowl?"

Dad shook his head. "No. Because you haven't stopped smiling since he joined us."

My father walked over to Maddox, giving him a fist bump. Throughout the game, they'd talked about technique. I could tell my father was impressed with Maddox' skill, which was no small feat. Mom seemed to like him too. She'd asked him several questions about his life. Ever the educator, she'd been curious about his education. I was shocked to find out he'd dropped out of college as a freshman and never went back. I figured that would be a huge strike against him in my mother's eyes, but she'd surprised me when she admitted that college wasn't for everyone. And LJ? Maddox had said the magic words early on—Detroit Pistons fan. From there, the two had plenty to talk about.

When the game ended with me once again in last place and Maddox in first, we packed up our stuff and said our good-byes. For dinner, we decided on Vinology, a restaurant and wine bar on Main Street in downtown Ann Arbor.

"I thought you weren't drinking today?" Maddox asked.

I peered at him over the rim of my wine glass. "So you *were* listening."

"Not entirely. I kind of tuned out the flirtatious vibe you had with ol' boy."

"You caught that too, huh?"

"But you turned him down when he asked for a date."

I twisted my glass. "I did."

He pinned me with his intense stare. "Why?"

"I think you know why."

"Maybe I just want to hear you say it."

We'd segued easily from topic to topic during dinner. As we dined, I found myself wishing the night wouldn't end. Maddox was so funny. He had a dry sense of humor that cracked me up. What I enjoyed most was that he was honest, direct. He didn't talk over me, but he didn't let me monopolize the conversation either. He was engaged—and *engaging*.

"I couldn't imagine spending more time with Carl," I admitted. "He was attractive, but..." I held his gaze. "He wasn't you."

After he paid the bill, we walked down Main Street. It was still early, so Ann Arbor was still buzzing with activity. The Christmas lights brightened the way, off in the distance carolers were singing "Angels We Have Heard on High," one of my favorite songs once upon a time.

"So you only drink Dr. Pepper when you're with your father?" he asked.

I hunched a shoulder. "Mostly. He's a recovering addict, so we make an effort not to partake when we're around him.

Even though, he'd never ask us to do so. It's kind of like a tribute to him and everything he's been through."

"I like that. My mother hated the taste of alcohol, so we would crack open the sparkling cider for dinner."

"Why?"

"Reminded her of her parents. She would always lecture me about my beer habit."

I giggled. "Speaking of... You ordered an exotic beer when we first met. And I can't remember the name to save my life."

He grinned. "No telling. Ten years ago, I'd just started getting into craft beer. It could've been anything."

"It's funny how memory works. One small detail can eclipse a wealth of larger ones."

He eyed me curiously. "Are we still talking about beer?"

"Not really. Just thinking about how this is the first Christmas season that I've enjoyed in a long time."

"I wasn't aware you didn't like the holidays."

For years, I'd abhorred December because the month was a reminder of my failure. Yuletide, carols, trees, and even snow reminded of my wedding, my divorce, and my fucked-up marriage. "My ex was a Christmas nut," I explained. "He insisted we marry during the season because it was his favorite time of year. I thought that meant he was a good guy because what *bad* guy liked Christmas, right?"

"What happened between you two?"

"He was a cheater." Marv's wandering eye hadn't been a secret when I agreed to marry him. I'd just pushed all doubts aside so that I could be with him. "When I met you, I'd just discovered a text from the woman he'd eventually leave me for. Little Miss Christmas."

Maddox frowned. "Because she likes Christmas too?"

I let out a humorless chuckle. "I guess you could say that, but she was actually crowned Little Miss Christmas in elementary school. I couldn't stand her, but I thought I loved him.

On the wedding day, I knew I was making a big mistake and I cried... But then I married him anyway."

"You were young. Nothing wrong with wanting to believe the best in someone."

"Except he was never the best, and I'd fooled myself into thinking he would change. I threw myself into the marriage, twisted myself in knots to please him. Since he loved Christmas, I made sure we did it big every year. Parties, decorations, cookies, music... All day, every day."

Then, one day, Marv had come home from work and told me wanted a divorce, but he wouldn't get one because the church elder told him he had to stay with me. He'd confessed that he'd never stopped seeing that bitch and made it clear that he didn't want me anymore. Because *I* wasn't wife material, because *I* didn't want to have a threesome, because *I* worked too much. Because *I*, because *I* because *I*... Everything was my fault.

"I left him," I said. "Took my shit and walked away. But I've dreaded this season every year since because it was a reminder of everything I'd lost."

"Damn," Maddox murmured. "Is he still around because I want to kick the shit out of him."

I laughed. "If he saw you, he'd run. Muthafuckin' punk."

"If I see him, he better run."

I searched Maddox' eyes, noted the sincerity in his brown orbs. Stepping on the tips of my toes, I kissed him, sucking his bottom lip until he groaned and pulled me closer. I wrapped my arms around his neck. "I'm ready for the second course."

Half an hour later, Maddox carried me into his Airbnb, his mouth fused to mine. We didn't stop to take our shoes off, my belt bag was still pushed up into my breasts, and my coat was hanging off one shoulder as he walked us to the bedroom.

Inside the bedroom, he set me on my feet and turned me away from him. He peeled my coat off, kissing my earlobe, the back of my neck, my shoulder. My belt bag was next, tossed somewhere behind us. My shirt followed, then my bra. His warm lips traveled down my spine, and back up again.

Shit. Maddox hadn't even touched my breasts or my clit, his dick was still inside his pants, and my body was on fire, already on the brink of an orgasm. He unbuttoned my jeans, unzipped my zipper, and slid his hand inside my panties. I gasped when his finger brushed my clit, I moaned when he strummed it like a guitar, and I groaned when he slipped one, then two fingers inside my pussy. *Oh. My. God.*

He groaned. "It's okay, Sloane," he whispered against my ear. "Come."

Damn. Maybe it was his words, or the low sound of his voice in my ear. It could've been the heat of his body behind me, the feel of his erection against my back, the press of his fingers against my spot that sent me over the edge. But as my orgasm pulsed through me stealing my breath and my soul, I decided it was all of the above.

Sated, I wanted to sink to the floor, but his hold on me prevented it. "Shoes," he murmured, nipping my shoulder.

The low command registered through the haze of desire, and I kicked off my UGGs. He pushed my jeans down, then my panties, kissing the small of my back, my ass, the backs of my thighs and my knees.

I tried to remain standing. I really tried. My legs didn't cooperate, though, and my knees buckled under the pleasure. Only I didn't fall. Instead, he scooped me up in his arms, carried me to the bed, and dropped me on the soft mattress.

Opening my eyes, I laughed. "Thanks," I breathed.

The corner of his mouth quirked up. "No problem." He tugged his shirt off.

"Ooo wee." My eyes widened as I realized I'd said that out loud.

He chuckled. "You're funny."

"Damn, Maddox. Do you live in the gym?"

He barked out a laugh and climbed on top of me. "Sometimes," he murmured against my mouth. He licked my lips, before he kissed me, and...

Lawd, he is so damn hot. I unbuckled his jeans and pushed them off his hips as his lips brushed over my jaw, down my neck, over my collarbone, and finally my breasts. He sucked a nipple in his mouth and I... Okay, I whimpered. Because it felt too damn good, *we* felt too fucking right to hold it in.

Maddox had seemingly made it his mission to drive me crazy with need for him, because he continued his journey down my body, dipping his tongue in my belly button and licking his way to my pussy. I raised myself up on my elbows because I wanted to watch. Yet, when his tongue flicked over my clit before he sucked it into his mouth, I fell back against the mattress. And, yes, I whimpered again because it was sweet torture. The way he seemed to know what I needed at every turn. This orgasm crashed into me, sharp and intense. *So good*.

I trembled when I felt his tongue on my clit again, and I closed my legs around his head. "You're killing me," I whispered.

"I'm still hungry," he murmured before he brought me to yet another orgasm under his tongue.

My eyes drifted closed as waves of pleasure rolled through me. But Maddox wasn't done. No, he was on the move again, kissing his way back up my body, lingering at my breasts before his lips met mine again. *His mouth*... I could probably die happy if I could kiss him every day.

That thought sobered me and I tensed up for a quick second because... That's not what this was. *Right*?

"Hey?" he called softly. "You okay?"

I searched his eyes. Ten years ago, I'd made the decision to sleep with a stranger because he didn't feel strange to me. He was sincere, sweet. When I looked at him now, I realized that hadn't changed. That thing that drew me to him, that made me feel safe with him was still there. I still wanted to immerse myself in it, in him.

I traced his jaw with my finger, kissed his full lips. Wrapping my legs around his waist, I said, "I'm perfect."

His expression softened. "You are that." He circled my nose with his before sealing his lips to mine again. I heard the rustle of a wrapper and realized he'd somehow managed to remember the condom. Good thing because I could barely remember my name. He ripped the wrapper with his teeth, sheathed himself and captured my bottom lip again as he pushed inside me.

Shit.

We both said it at the same time, which made me laugh. But when I looked at Maddox, there was no hint of a smile on his face. Only heat.

"Maddox." I gasped as he thrust deeper.

My ability to think about anything other than his dick had evaporated under the power of his thrusts. The slow and easy pace coupled with the heat of his gaze was almost too much to bear. Tears sprang to my eyes, it felt so damn good. *Too good*.

Another orgasm crested within me, and I cursed it. Because I wanted to hold on to this feeling, to him. I wanted to bottle this feeling, to store it in a place that I could revisit often.

He ghosted his lips over my ear before he bit down on it lightly. "Let go," he commanded softly. "We have all night."

The fact that he'd known what I was thinking was a question for another day because my body demanded a release. I fell over, groaning his name over and over, pleading with him to never stop. A moment later, he followed me over, letting out a low, long growl.

We stayed like that for a while, bodies intertwined, foreheads pressed together. He kissed my brow, the tip of my nose, then my lips before rolling over onto his back. I snuggled into him, still needing the connection.

Wrapping my arms around his waist, I sighed. I wanted to say something, I wanted to confess. Over the years, I'd dreamed of him. I'd wished for him. It wasn't every day, but he would sneak into my mind and my thoughts when I'd least expect it. During a movie or while I was brushing my teeth, or even in the shower. Sometimes I'd hear his voice when I was cooking or running or hanging a painting. *Did he feel the same way?*

I squeezed my eyes shut, willing myself to stop thinking about him as if we were a real thing. The facts were clear. While Maddox was here now, he wasn't mine. And I would do well to remember that.

"Sloane?"

I lifted myself up on my elbow. "Huh?"

A lazy smile spread over his lips and my stomach tightened. "What do you think about dessert?"

I laughed, straddling him. "I think that's the best idea you've had all night."

CHAPTER 7

Christmas Spirit

MADDOX

When I was younger, I could never fall asleep at a decent time on Christmas Eve. Maybe it was the prospect of gifts or the promise of good food, but I would spend most of the night staring up at the ceiling, waiting for the sun to come up. For some reason, my mother always knew I was struggling because she'd poke her head in my room to check on me. As I got older, I purposefully waited for her late-night visit. Sometimes we ate cookies. Other times we'd watch a movie. She'd even play a video game or two some years. The gesture meant everything to me.

Before she died, she called me to her room because she was too weak to visit my room. While it wasn't Christmas Eve, it felt like it because it was our last perfect night together. We'd talked, shared a plate of sugar cookies, and watched her favorite movie, "Miracle on 34th Street." And then we'd fallen asleep. Two days later, she was gone.

Between my family and Sloane, I'd done a pretty good job of staying busy leading up to tonight. Taylar had packed my schedule with family time. Earlier, Sloane and I had ventured out to the Detroit Zoo and walked the *Wild Lights* trail. Then, we'd had dinner at a new restaurant in Royal Oak, Michigan. Even with all the activity, today had been a struggle.

Although I'd tried to get out of it, Olivia had insisted I spend the night with them. It had been years since I'd slept in the same house with my family. The tension between Broderick and I made it slightly uncomfortable, but I'd decided to make the most of my time there.

My phone buzzed. I reached over and grabbed it from the nightstand.

Sloane: *Go to sleep.*

About an hour ago, I'd texted her that I couldn't sleep, but she hadn't responded so I'd assumed she was knocked out. I typed my reply: *How did you know I was still up?*

Sloane: I didn't know, but you replied to my text, so my original message still applies.

I asked her what she was still doing up, and then my phone rang. This time, it was a FaceTime request. Smiling, I accepted. Damn, she was a sight for sore eyes, even in her head scarf. "Hey," I said.

"It was easier to call." She held up Scotch Tape and a pair of scissors. "I'm wrapping gifts."

"See, you should've bought gift cards," I told her. Unlike Taylar, Sloane agreed with my view on gift cards, but she'd decided to step her game up this year. "You could've saved so much time."

"I told you... I wanted to switch it up." She frowned in concentration as she cut the paper. "Besides, my niece and

72

nephews are too little to appreciate a gift card. They want toys and video games."

"I wanted that new PlayStation myself."

She groaned. "Don't tell me you're a gamer."

I chuckled. "I play from time to time."

She ripped a piece of tape off the dispenser and shook her head. "Figures."

"What did you ask for?"

Sloane glanced at me. "Money."

"Seriously?"

She winked. "No. I didn't ask for anything. My mother will probably buy me some bras and socks, and my father will give me cash like he does every year. You know... one year she gave us a huge thing of toilet paper for Christmas. Best. Gift. Ever."

Cracking up, I said, "Now that's a good gift. TP is expensive as hell."

"Right? What was your favorite Christmas gift?"

I didn't have to think about it. The year I'd declared I wanted to be a photographer, Mom surprised me with a 35mm camera. "A compact camera," I replied. "And film."

Sloane smiled. "I bet you thought you were the shit."

"Nobody could tell me anything."

"Do you still have it?"

My vision blurred as memories of my mother flashed through my mind. The first picture I'd taken with that camera was of her, opening the gift I'd bought her from Santa's Secret Shop at my school. I still carried that photo with me, tucked away in my wallet to remind me of how far I'd come. "I do," I answered finally.

"Does it still work?"

"I have no idea," I admitted. "It's hidden away in a safe place. What about you? Was toilet paper really the best gift you've ever received?"

Sloane pointed at the screen. "No. It was the Barbie Townhouse. I wanted the Dream House, but my mother nixed that idea."

"So you were a Barbie girl?"

"Absolutely. I had so many dolls. I must've played with them for hours every day, thinking of elaborate stories. Ken and Barbie used to get busy often."

I barked out a laugh. "What?"

"Yes. Ken didn't have a dick, but I pretended it was there."

This woman was... Everything. I could spend hours just listening to her talk. "You're silly."

She shrugged. "I can only be me." We didn't talk for a few minutes while she finished wrapping her second gift. When she was done, she looked at me. "Are you okay?"

I could've lied and said I was good. But I didn't want to start a trend of hiding my feelings with her. Especially since she'd been honest with me. "I'm trying to be."

"It's okay if you're not."

I sucked in a deep breath and let it out slowly. "I know she's in a better place, but I hate that she's not here."

"I can't pretend to know what you're going through. But I do know one thing. Your mother *is* here, Maddox. She's in that camera she bought you for Christmas. She's in the cards she gave you for your birthdays. She's in her pound cake recipe. She lives in you. She has a permanent place in your heart, and no one can take that away from you."

Tears burned my eyes. Sloane was right. My mother believed wholeheartedly that God didn't make mistakes. And she'd trusted Him. Now, it was time for me to do the same. "Thanks, Sloane."

"Anytime."

"Does this mean, I can always call you in the middle of the night when I can't sleep?"

She snorted. "Don't get carried away. I need my beauty

sleep. I get so mean if I don't get it in."

"What else is new?" I joked.

Her mouth fell open. "I wish I was next to you because I would thump you."

"What? You said you would *hump* me if you were here?"

Her head fell back as she laughed. "You're stupid. Stop making me laugh. It's too late for this shit. Full disclosure, though. I probably *would* hump you if I was there." My eyes felt heavy, but I didn't want to hang up. "Maddox?"

"Huh?"

"You should get some sleep. You look tired."

"I'm not sleepy. Just resting for a minute."

She giggled. "Yes, you are. And that's perfectly okay."

"I wanted to hear about your favorite Christmas movie."

"I'll tell you tomorrow when you come over for dessert."

I yawned. "I could always come tuck you in tonight."

She flashed a wicked smirk. "Careful. I might just let you."

I closed my eyes. "Just say the word."

"I only have two words for you, Mr. Cross. Good night."

My eyes popped open, but she'd already hung up. Seconds later, a new text popped up. A smile tugged on my lips as I read her text: *Go to sleep. Merry Christmas, Maddox.*

And I did just that.

Several hours later, I awoke to loud voices and the smell of bacon. It took a few moments, but I finally made my way down the stairs. The sight of my father dancing with Olivia to Nat King Cole's version of "The Christmas Song" in the kitchen made me smile. They greeted me with hugs.

Taylar was standing at the stove stirring grits. I swiped a piece of bacon from the platter on the kitchen island and gave my sister a hug. Then, I joined Ryker at the table. "Merry Christmas, bruh," I said.

Ryker wished me the same. "You good?"

I nodded. "I'm good."

Olivia brought the waffles over to the table. The years had been good to her. She still looked as young as she did when I met her. Probably because she worked out five days a week and taught a Pilates class for seniors. Smiling at me, she cupped my cheek. "So handsome." She kissed my cheek. "I made plenty of salmon croquettes for you."

I rubbed my hands together. "That's what I've been waiting for."

Dad set a fruit tray down and took a strawberry from it, popping it in his mouth. "Ryker, go grab your brother. It's time to eat."

I'd been there since around nine o'clock last night, and I'd yet to see Broderick. I'd heard him, though—*and* the argument between him and Dad.

Broderick entered the kitchen, fully dressed, coat on. "No need. I won't be staying for breakfast."

Olivia whirled around. "What?"

"Broderick, no," Taylar said. "It's Christmas."

"It's best that I leave." Broderick glared at me. "This house is too crowded anyway."

"What is your problem?" Dad roared. "You walk around like you don't have to answer to anybody or anything, and I'm sick of it. You will show some respect to me, your mother, and *all* of your siblings. If you can't do that, then it probably *is* best you get the hell out of my house."

Olivia grabbed Dad's arm. "Ryan, please. Stop."

I met Ryker's murderous gaze but didn't say anything. He did, though. "Man, sit your ass down. Mom only asked one thing of you, and you can't even do that."

Broderick glanced at me again with cold, hard eyes. "You got something to say too?"

It took everything in me not to wear his ass out. But I

wouldn't do that to Olivia. "No," I told him. Then, I thought better of it. "Actually, I do. Your mother is still here, breathing, wanting to spend time with you. Trust me, you don't want the alternative. Instead of being grateful for the gift of more time, you're acting like the selfish asshole you've always been. I don't care if you don't like me, and I don't care if you don't like yourself. But show her the love and grace that she's always shown you and everyone else here.

I glanced around at the stunned faces of my family. No one said anything, they simply took their seats at the table— Broderick included. Dad blessed the food and we started eating. For several moments, the only sound in the room was the clinking of silverware against Olivia's holiday china.

Taylar finally broke the ice when she said, "The good news is I didn't burn the grits this year." She laughed. "That's something, right?"

Ryker cracked up first, then like dominoes, we all fell over with laughter.

After the blow-up at breakfast, we spent the rest of the day in neutral corners—Broderick on one side and everybody else on the other. Olivia had dinner catered and we all ate in the family room while we watched the football game. We'd just finished opening gifts when, for some stupid-ass reason, Taylar wanted to relive her childhood and play Operation.

An hour later, Taylar swept the board off the table. "Dammit, you always win."

"That's 'cause I'm the best," I teased.

Rolling her eyes, Tay said, "Whatever. Rematch."

"Nah, sis." I finished my sweet potato pie and stood, dropping my napkin on my plate. "I have plans."

Olivia intercepted me on my way to the kitchen to toss my plate. "Maddox? Can I see you for a moment in my office?"

I stopped off in the kitchen, then went to Olivia's home office. It was clear they'd done a substantial renovation to the house since the last time I'd been there, and the office space was no exception. Simple artwork hung on the walls and the furniture was simple, sleek. Not the heavy wood and big pieces that were there before. She'd also added a few feminine accents. The modern décor reminded me of Sloane, and I wondered what she would think of it. She'd shown me a few of her designs, and she had the same taste.

Instead of taking a seat, I walked over to the window. Olivia had a view of their garden and the new gazebo in the backyard. The Christmas lights gave it an ethereal glow and I couldn't look away. *Mom would've loved it.*

"I love it out there," Olivia said, approaching me. She stared outside. "It's so peaceful. Even in the winter." She chuckled.

I swallowed hard. "I can see why."

"I called you back here because we haven't really had much time to talk, and I wanted to give you something." She handed me a wrapped gift. "I thought it would be best if you opened it in private."

I made no move to open the gift, though, because I had a feeling it would make me emotional. And I'd told myself that I wasn't going to cry today.

"Maddox?" Olivia called, pulling me from my thoughts. "I'll never be able to replace your mother, and I wouldn't try. But I love you like I gave birth to you, and I made her a promise to be there for you, to take care of you. I intend to keep that promise.

The first tear fell, then the dam broke. "You talked to my mom?" I asked.

"We talked often. One of the things I never did was blame your mother for Ryan's actions. We weren't together when he met your mother. And when I did take him back, I took him back knowing that you were going to be a part of our lives. I wouldn't change that for anything in this world. You are my son, just like Broderick, just like Ryker."

My throat was thick with emotion, but I finally opened the gift. Inside was a framed picture of the three of us—me, Mom, and Olivia. I remembered the day well. My first photo exhibit at a local gallery in Charleston. I brushed it with my thumb, over my mother's face. We were smiling, happy. Mom and Olivia had their arms wrapped around me, holding me. The symbolism of the image was almost too much to bear, but I loved it all the same.

I met Olivia's teary eyes. "Thank you," I whispered.

"You're welcome, baby. Whenever you look at this picture, know that I've got you—*we've* got you." She pulled me into her warm embrace. And I let her. "I love you, son."

"I love you too, Ma."

Olivia insisted I eat another slice of pie before I went to Sloane's house. I didn't know how I'd eat another piece of food for the rest of today, and tomorrow too. But I would do my damn best to eat Sloane's dessert.

I knocked on the door and waited. The door swung open, and Sloane was standing there in a Santa hat and, pretty much, nothing else. My gaze raked over her body, from her stilettos to her lace panties to her fur-trimmed red bustier. *Shit*.

She smirked. "Ready for dessert?" She leaned in and kissed me, grazing my bottom lip with her teeth before tracing it with her tongue.

"Hell yeah."

Holding up her phone, she played some remixed TikTok song and said, "Then, bring that dick here."

I tugged her to me and lifted her over my shoulder, smacking her ass lightly. She cracked up, and as soon as I entered her place, she slammed the door shut.

CHAPTER 8

Warm Hands, Warm Feet, Warm Heart

MADDOX

I can't get enough of her.

Every night I dreamed of her. I wanted her every hour, every minute, every second of every damn day. Christmas had come and gone, and we were speeding toward New Year's Day and, eventually, my departure date. And I found myself in the peculiar position of *not* wanting to leave.

The sound of my zipper being released echoed in the room. "Sloane," I groaned, burying my fingers in her hair. Her tiny hand slid inside my boxer briefs and closed around my dick. "Fuck."

She licked me from base to tip, keeping her eyes on me, watching me. Slowly, she wrapped her lips around me and sucked me in. Her eyes fluttered closed as she repeated the motion—over and over again. *Damn.*

I pressed into her, transfixed as she worked. The way her tongue brushed against me, the feel of her warm mouth around me, the amount of suction she used, the sounds she made... *Damn*. She looked so perfect with her mouth around my dick that I wanted to capture the image with my camera. And the fact that she looked like she was enjoying it? *Shit, I'm going to come*.

A few curse words, a grunt, and a low groan was all I could manage. I wanted to tell her to stop, that I wanted to be inside her when I came, but her eyes popped open and she shook her head slightly, signaling that she didn't plan on stopping. So, I let go, coming so long and so hard that I could barely breathe.

Sloane licked me again, a wicked gleam in her eyes. And I... was once again wrecked by the woman in front of me. I tugged her to her feet and kissed her, pouring everything into the kiss. I fell back on the bed, pulling her with me and rolling her onto her back. "I can't get enough of you." I nipped at her chin, then kissed my way to her breasts. I tugged on her nipple with my teeth before sucking it into my mouth.

She groaned. "Doc."

The nickname was new, something she'd started calling me yesterday actually. I loved it. I pushed inside her, fusing my mouth to hers again. There was something about the way we moved together, the way we fit together.

She wrapped her legs around my waist and brushed her finger over my jaw. I sensed she wanted to say something, but she didn't speak. I didn't question it either. We made slow, quiet love this time. The only sounds that registered were the hum of the ceiling fan and the pounding of my heart in my ear. We came at the same time, our mouths sealed together, our bodies clinging to each other.

After a moment, I circled her nose with mine and rolled over on my back, pulling her with me. She swept her hand over my chest and purred. "I'm tempted to keep you," she said.

Her words gave me pause because there really was no good reason she couldn't. Other than the fact that we'd never discussed what happens next. "Would it be a bad thing to keep me?" Silence stretched on and I wondered what she was thinking. "Sloane?"

"Hmm?"

My stomach roiled and a heaviness settled in my chest. "What's on your mind?"

"Work," she grumbled, sitting up. "I have a lot of shit to catch up on."

Sloane wasn't a liar, so it bothered me that she felt the need to lie. "I thought you were taking some time off?" I challenged.

She glanced around the room, looking everywhere but at me. "What did you do with my underwear?"

Again, she'd ignored my question. "You could always stay," I suggested. We'd slept together several times, but the only time we'd spent the entire night together was Christmas. Since then, there was always an excuse, a reason to leave. "It's the middle of the night, Sloane."

She slumped forward and let out a heavy sigh. "Maddox... I'm sorry. I have to go." She slid off the bed, pulling the comforter with her and wrapping it around her body. As she searched for her things, I watched her. Waited for her to say something else. Apparently, she was going to pretend I hadn't asked her a couple of questions. "Ah, there it is." She picked up her dress and walked into the bathroom. Several minutes later, she emerged, fully dressed. Her hair was combed, and she'd even put on fresh lip gloss.

"Are you going home? Or to the bar?" That came out more accusatory than I'd intended, but fuck it. I was pissed.

She turned to me, a smile on her face. "The bar? Why would I go to the bar?"

I shrugged. "I don't know, why would you?"

"Maddox." She climbed onto the bed and kissed me. "I'm just going home, okay?" I stared at her, but didn't comment. "Fine, you asked if it would be so bad if I kept you?"

"And you acted like I didn't say anything," I said.

"Because it's... The point is I can't keep you. Do you really think this can go anywhere? You live in South Carolina, and I'm not moving. My life is here, and I wouldn't ask you to leave *your* life for me. I've enjoyed being with you, spending time getting to know you. I don't want to see you leave, but you will. So..."

"That's it?" I finished for her. "No conversation about it."

"I thought we were talking about it now, but maybe I'll stop by tomorrow after my last two dates."

My body tensed. "Wait, what? I thought you were done with that."

"I never said that. Look, it's not going anywhere, so—"

"So don't go."

"I told you... It's the principle." She sighed. "Can we talk about it tomorrow night? Over dinner?"

"Let me think about it," I said, throwing her own words back at her.

She flinched visibly. "Okay." She scooted off the bed and grabbed her purse. "I'll talk to you later."

Later that morning, I met my father for breakfast. "What's up, Dad?" I gave him a hug. "Sorry I'm late."

Dad grinned. "No problem. I ordered orange juice and biscuits."

"Cool."

"How are you, son?"

It had been hours since Sloane left my rental, and we hadn't spoken since. No texts, no FaceTiming, no calls. Which was strange since we'd talked multiple times a day since bowling. "Good," I lied.

True to form, my father called me out on it. "When did you start lying to me?"

I dropped my head and apologized. "I'm just in a foul mood."

Dad chuckled. "Been there. Yesterday, actually."

"Everything okay?" I asked.

"Just campaign stuff. Olivia and I were wondering if you would shoot pictures for our event next month."

I'd been working as a photographer for many years, but this was the first time my father had asked me to work with his campaign. "You know I don't like those people."

Laughing, Dad shook his head. "I don't either, son. But it's a necessary evil. Think you can do that for me?"

I agreed. "Let me know the dates and I'll plan to come back."

"So what *are* your plans? I must admit we enjoyed having you around. I hope you know that you can always come home. You can stay at the house until you find a place of your own. Save the money on the rental."

My father was speaking to a part of me that was very interested in being near family. I'd considered a move multiple times, but I'd yet to settle on anything concrete. I just knew that Charleston was no longer home. "Been thinking about it," I admitted. "But I need to take some time and figure out what effect a move here will have on my career."

"I definitely understand, son. We haven't always agreed, but you've done well for yourself. I'm proud of you, and I want you closer. So if I have some sway, I vote for Michigan."

"We'll see."

"Taylar told me you were seeing someone here."

"Tay talks too much," I grumbled.

"Is it true?"

"Somewhat." I told my father about Sloane, starting at our first meeting and ending with our last conversation. Of course,

I kept it PG, and downplayed the emotional *and* physical aspects, but he got the gist.

"So you like this woman?"

Like felt extremely inadequate, but I was hesitant to say it was more than that, so I nodded.

"Well, the best thing I've ever done was fight for my marriage," he said. "If you care about Sloane, don't let her walk away without telling her how you feel. Let her know how important she is to you."

"Don't you think it's too soon to be making declarations? We barely know each other."

"You can't control everything, son. I met Olivia on a Sunday, and by Friday, I knew I wanted to marry her. Sometimes things just happen fast, and you have to decide if you're going to shit or get off the pot."

I laughed. "You said *shit*, Dad."

"I say a lot of things when Olivia isn't around. You'll understand one day."

My father hadn't said anything that I didn't already feel in my heart. I didn't know how it happened, but I knew beyond the shadow of a doubt, that I couldn't let her walk away—not without a fight.

***

SLOANE

"You know you fucked up, right?"

I glared at my sister. She'd said that about six times since I'd told her about my conversation with Maddox. "Stop saying that."

"I'll keep saying it until you admit that you fucked up."

85

Courtney and I were sitting at one of our favorite local bars, The Ice Box, waiting on my last two dates. Forty more minutes of wasted time because, at this point, no man would be able to measure up to Maddox. We'd spent less than three weeks total together and I'd never felt so free, so comfortable, so invested in a man. Everything had happened so fast, though. *Too fast*? Could it be the real thing? *Am I just horny*?

Even as I thought that, I knew there was more to us than sex, than physical attraction. It was innate, like we were meant to be like this with each other. I felt it ten years ago. *I feel it now*.

"Sloane?" Courtney shifted in her seat to face me. "I'm going to be honest with you. We never expected you to like any of these dates. At least, *I* didn't. Well, except for the Architect and the Pilot."

I frowned. "What?"

"Richard the Funeral Director? Come on, did you really think we thought he was a good fit?"

"So why did you do it?"

"Because you needed to get out of your own way. You had to see what you don't want, to know what you need. It was never about finding you a forever boo. If you decide to stay single because that's what you want, go for it. I just don't want you to stay single because you don't want to get hurt, or because you *got* hurt. You've made a lot of boss moves, including walking away from that toxic asshole. Trust yourself. You got this."

I sagged in relief and let her words settle in my heart. Courtney had always been my take-no-shit big sister. To hear that she thought *I* was a boss, made me feel good. "You've certainly put a lot of things in perspective, though. I'm glad to hear you didn't really think the Teeth Guy was perfect for me."

She threw her head back, cracking up. "Girl!" She clapped.

"That was hilarious. Bliss had us rolling giving us the play-by-play of that date."

"I'm also glad y'all heffas were able to laugh at my expense."

"We'll have material for years off that shit."

"Guess this means you're going to Disney with me?"

Courtney waved a dismissive hand. "Girl, bye. I'm not going to no Disney World. You're still going, but you can pick your own guest."

I leaned back in my chair. "I have to thank you, though," I said. "Without this journey, I probably would've embraced my inner Ms. Scroogette forever. I definitely would've never faced my past because it was easier to keep the wall up. This process wasn't really about the dates, and I understand that now. I still have some work to do, but I'm ready to let myself off the hook for my failed relationship."

"Aw." Her chin trembled. "That's good, sweetie. I'm proud of you."

"What do I do about Maddox?"

"Talk to him?" she suggested. "I know it's super fast, like lightning fast. Like whirlwind fast. Like—"

"Okay, I get it." I cut her off. "Trust me. It's hasn't even been a month."

"Not even three weeks, really," she added.

I glared at her.

She smiled. "Just kidding. Look, I saw you two together and I'm convinced there is something worth pursing there. Don't sabotage it before it even gets started."

My alarm went off and I sighed. "I guess it's time to get this over with." I stood. "Wait, since you were playing me this whole time, do I have to go on these last two dates?"

Courtney pushed me. "Go. Just get it over with."

I took a seat at a table near the bar. My phone buzzed, and I read the incoming text.

Bliss: *Please put some lip gloss on.*

Frowning, I glanced around the bar. Courtney was still sitting alone, looking down at her phone and typing furiously. I craned my neck to check behind the bar. No Bliss, no Blake, and no Dallas. Curious, I typed: *Where are you*?

Her response came seconds later: *Don't worry about it. Just do it. And fix your hair, chile.*

I did as I was told, applying a fresh coat of lip gloss and smoothing a hand over my head. I checked my reflection in my compact and dropped everything back in my purse.

"Is this seat taken?"

My head popped up, surprised to see Maddox standing there looking like a dark chocolate treat. "What are you... How did you know I was here?"

He sat down across from me. "I had a little help."

I knew it. I leaned forward. "Tonight, or the whole time?"

"The whole time," he told me. "Bliss has been giving me all of your date information. It was up to me to decide when or *if* I wanted to show up."

I shook my head. "That girl... I had a feeling she was behind this."

"She's good at what she does," he said with a shrug. "I can see why she's a successful matchmaker."

"I know. She gets on my nerves, but I love her to death."

A short guy approached the table timidly. "Are you Sloane Wilson?"

Maddox glanced over his shoulder at the man. A wide smile spread across his lips. "She definitely is," he said.

"Hi," the stranger held out his hand, "I'm Jordan. My mother goes to the same church as Bliss' parents."

I didn't shake Jordan's hand, but I did greet him with a smile. "Hi."

Jordan eyed Maddox tentatively. "Should I come back?"

"No," Maddox and I said simultaneously. Then, we both laughed.

Maddox turned to Jordan. "She's good, man. You can go now."

Jordan backed away slowly, never taking his eyes off Maddox. "Okay. It was nice to meet you, Sloane."

I waved at him. "You too. Bye." The poor guy practically ran out of the bar. "I think you scared him."

"He should be scared," Maddox said. "Trying to date my girl."

I love the sound of that. Because I was certainly *his* girl. "I do have another date, though."

"No you don't," he informed. "You're done. I'm dates nine and ten. And eleven. And twelve. And every other date after that."

"Are you sure about that?" I folded my arms over my chest. "You know I prefer twenty-minutes dates. Will that be enough time for you?"

He smirked. "I can get the job done in twenty. But I do like to take my time."

The promise in his eyes made me want to pull him out of there and let him give me a sample in his rental car. But I said, "Sounds good. I think I can pencil you in. Before we skip to the main course, though, can I say something?"

"What is it?"

"I hate to point out the obvious, but you still live in South Carolina."

"For now."

"What exactly does that mean?"

"It means I'm making changes. And I want those changes to involve you. Sloane," he picked up my hand and kissed my palm, "I want more time with you. I want nights, mornings, afternoons, evenings... I want everything. Because I'm pretty sure I'm falling for you, and I want you to fall with me."

I couldn't breathe. Because his words pulled me apart at the seams—in a good way. "You're pulling out all the stops," I breathed.

"I tend to do that when I want something." He tugged me gently, prompting me to walk around the table. I sat on his lap. "It's kind of crazy, right? When we met all those years ago, I had no idea I would be there today, laying my heart on the line. But I'm doing it because, for the first time in a while, I feel hope. I want to hold on to that."

Tears sprang to my eyes. "I know how you feel. I went into this season dreading it. Now I can listen to a Christmas song without feeling sick to my stomach. And now I can envision a future where I'm free to be who I am—and be happy. I'd like that future to include you."

"So does this mean you're going to let me date you?"

I tapped my chin. "Hmm… I'll think about it."

He narrowed his eyes. "Really?"

I laughed. "Okay, I thought about it and it's too late. I've already fallen, and there is no one else I want to date."

"Now that's what I wanted to hear." He kissed me, long and hard. And I didn't care who was watching because I wanted to be in his arms, I wanted to be with him. "Oh, and I'm going to Disney with you too."

"What if I don't want you to go?" I teased.

His gaze locked on mine. "Do you?"

Maddox had given me a reason to start again, and I didn't want to waste anymore time. "Only if you promise to take me to Cinderella Castle."

"I'll take you anywhere you want to go."

I brushed my lips over his. "For now, can we start with my bedroom?" I winked. "We'll figure the rest out later."

All my life, I'd heard the stories of all-consuming passion and love at first sight. My mother had bought my father at a sorority date auction for twenty-five dollars forty-plus years ago, and they're still together. I'd always thought they were the exception, though, not the rule. Now, I wasn't so sure. Even though everything was still new, I already couldn't imagine life without him. Maddox had brought magic back into my life— the magic of possibilities, the magic of a perfect kiss, the magic of meddling friends and family, the magic of a rekindled connection, the magic of Christmas, and the magic of love. And I couldn't wait to "date" him. Forever.

Epilogue

THE GIFT OF GOLD

SLOANE

February, Next Year

"Don't you think we should actually go to one of the theme parks?" Maddox swept a bar of soap over my stomach. "That is kind of the point, right?"

I leaned against his chest, closing my eyes as he washed me. We'd arrived at the resort yesterday and had yet to leave our suite. No Mickey, no Goofy, and definitely no Donald Duck. The only thing I wanted to do was immerse myself in my man. It had been a while since I'd seen him.

"Do we have to?" I asked, moaning when his finger brushed my nipple.

His low chuckle washed over me. "I promised to send a pic of you hugging Minnie Mouse—for Naija."

I grinned, thinking about my goddaughter. Even though I would do anything for her, I loathed the thought of venturing outside of this haven. "She'll be alright," I said.

He laughed. "You're silly."

I craned my neck up and kissed his chin. "I missed you."

Maddox had been in South Carolina for several weeks, getting everything in order to make the move to Ann Arbor. In that time, I'd only seem him once. I'd flown to Charleston to help him pack some of his mother's things.

Choosing Maddox, embracing our connection, had been the best decision I could've ever made. Every day I learned something else about him that made me... *love him*. It had only been a couple of months, but I knew I loved this man with everything in me. And it didn't scare me as much as I thought it would. It only made me better.

"It's okay, you know," he whispered, nipping my earlobe.

I frowned. "What?"

"You love me, and that's okay."

I froze, replaying the last few minutes in my head. How did he know what I was thinking? Had I said something out loud? Murmured something in my sleep? *Did I tell Bliss*? "Maddox, what are you talking about? Better yet, who you been talking to?"

"Nobody. Just you." He ran his thumb over my cheek. "I'll let you off the hook, though. I love you, Sloane."

I sat up straight, unfazed at the water splashing onto the floor. I turned to him, and he pulled me closer, wrapping my legs around his waist. I bit down on my bottom lip. "You do?"

He nodded, a smirk forming on his perfect lips. "I do." He kissed me, long and hard. "So much."

I sucked in a deep breath. "Okay." I twisted one of his locs. "That's nice."

"Nice?" He squeezed me until I cracked up. "Is that all it is?"

I wrapped my arms around his massive shoulders. "I don't know... Let me think about it."

He chuckled. "Think fast."

"Okay, okay." I searched his eyes. "I love you too." I dropped my head onto his shoulder.

"I know," he told me, hugging me to him. "Now, hop on this dick and then we'll go see Minnie Mouse."

I cracked up, but did as I was told, moaning when he gripped my hips and pushed himself inside me. "I think it's a date."

About those Youngs...

Did you enjoy Bliss Young and her sisters?

The Young Family have appeared in several of my other novels/novellas.

Paityn Young found everlasting love in my Park Manor novella, HER LITTLE SECRET. The twins, Blake and Bliss made their first appearance in her story.

Blake Young appeared again as Ryleigh's friend in my Once Upon a Baby novella, BEYOND EVER AFTER.

Duke Young burst onto the scene in my Pure Talent novels, THE WAY YOU TEMPT ME and THE WAY YOU HOLD ME. And he stole the show.

Dallas Young made her presence known in my Once Upon a Funeral novella, FINDING COOPER.

Then... The Young in Love Series kicked off with Blake's story, IT'S NOT ME, IT'S YOU. Next, Dallas found her happily every after in IT'S NOT LOVE, IT's BUSINESS.

Please Note: Several of these stories take place around the same time. Some events may happen in multiple books from a different POV.

www.ellewright.com

IT'S NOT
ME, IT'S
You

YOUNG
in love

She has a
license to
be petty.

Elle Wright

I fake laugh every time I think about how ironic it is to be a commitment-phobe relationship therapist who is also the daughter of two world-renowned marriage and family counselors. Seriously, it's comical!

Want to know how I messed up my life? Getting arrested for stealing a priceless artifact for a tearful client.

Want to know what my biggest problem is? Spending my life teaching women how to break relationships when all I want to do is make a relationship—with him.

Want to know what that makes me? The Break-Up Expert who is questioning everything I thought I knew.

Excerpt: *It's Not Me, It's You*

YOUNG IN LOVE, BOOK ONE

"Well?" A soft smack to my ass followed the question, pulling me from a peaceful slumber.

I couldn't open my eyes, though. I couldn't even stretch like I normally did when I woke from a much-needed nap. If I did either or both of those things, I'd give myself away. Because there was a man behind me, a penis inside me. And I'd actually fallen asleep—during sex. *There's a first for everything.*

Things had seemed promising tonight. Tasty food, sensual music, stimulating conversation. Dr. Donell Pointer had hit all my superficial checkmarks for consent. *Looks*. Sincere brown eyes, pretty white teeth, strong body. *Voice*. He sounded like hot sex on a smooth, dark chocolate stick. *Personality*. The good doctor had charisma. I'd laughed at his jokes and had even enjoyed a debate on why soulmates didn't exist. Of course, he'd landed on the they-do side of the fence, while I'd stayed firmly on the no-the-hell-they-don't side. I wasn't one of those women... I didn't believe in soulmates or that love-at-first-sight bullshit. The only way to fully love someone was if you *knew* them. Fight me. But even though he was a sappy son of a bitch, it was okay. Because he'd earned a check in my most important wet-panties category. *Smile*. Oh. My. God. That thing lit up the room. And the tiny creases around his full lips made my decision easy. Sex. All night, preferably. But at least two times.

Except, I couldn't get through *one* time without a smidge of drool on the pillow, and not because he'd knocked me out with his prowess. Dr. Donnell was definitely fine as hell. Too bad he had no fuck game. No back-breaking. No tongue-talking. No toe-curling orgasm. If brown liquor was the devil, there had to be a worse name for bad, boring, small-ass dick. Hell? Disappointment? Underwhelming? No, tragic? Yep, that's it.

"Blake?" His low voice broke my reverie.

Sighing, I opened my eyes slowly. *Damn*. Such a shame to be so hot, yet so limp. A nod and a forced smile later, I rolled over on my back and tried not to look at his *little* problem. "Where is my...?" I spotted my dress on the floor near the door. Before I could slide off the bed and race toward the bathroom, his hand wrapped around my wrist.

"Baby, where do you think you're going? I'm not done with you."

Oh, boy. I couldn't help the hard roll of my eyes. *Lord, I promise to do better and not be a hoe if you'll just get me out of here without me having to hurt this man's feelings*. He was a friend of a friend of an associate. The last thing I needed was friend-group gossip. "I have to leave. Early meeting." I offered him another smile and a light caress on his cheek.

He pulled me closer and nuzzled his nose against my neck. "How about you stay? We can have breakfast in the morning. Together."

Shit. He just said the magic, dirty word. *Together* was not what's up. "No need. I really have to go." I slipped out of his arms. But that hand of his remained on my wrist.

"I want to see you again. Maybe you'll give me a chance to change your mind about soulmates."

Like hell. "Not likely," I grumbled. "So, about that." I scratched my head, scrambled to find the right words. Somehow, "fuck off" seemed too harsh. "We don't have to do this. If you haven't realized yet, I'm not one of those women who needs the obligatory 'let's get together soon' speech." Shrugging, I continued, "It's probably best if we just not even try."

"Blake, you're a beautiful woman."

Can he just shut the hell up?

"I had a good time with you tonight." He brushed his thumb over my nipple.

I really have to find my panties.

Donnell rubbed his nose over my cheek and placed a chaste kiss there. "I don't want this to end."

Okay, I can live without my panties.

A mix between a groan and a whimper escaped his lips as he cupped my pussy in his palm—his *small* palm.

How the hell didn't I notice this?

"You're so beautiful," he whispered against my ear. "I want you."

Fuck the panties and the bra. I gripped his hand before his finger made contact with my clit. "Okay, stop. I'm done here." I pushed him away, stood, and picked up my dress.

"Blake?"

I rolled my eyes, slipping my dress on quickly. Luckily I'd chosen the comfortable, flowy maxi dress over the sexy, short black dress I'd considered wearing. Turning to him, I met his waiting, pitiful gaze. "Dr. Pointer, thanks for tonight. But I'm not interested in more of this." I motioned toward the bed. "It was..." I stopped short of saying it was nice, because I made it a habit not to lie. "Thanks for dinner and the...conversation."

Bolting from the room, I slammed the door shut and leaned against it to catch my breath. I ran my fingers through my probably fucked-up hair and hurried out of the hotel.

Acknowledgments

Woooo!!!! This book!!!

But God first! I want to thank Him for giving me this gift. And for loving me!

To my forever bae, Jason, thanks for being you. I love you so much.

To my #TRIBE, Angie, Sherelle, and Sheryl... When your sisters sprint with you even when they are done with their book, that's love! Thanks for having my back. Love y'all!!

Midnight, I can't thank you enough. You rock!

A special shout-out to the awesome readers , bloggers, and writers that I've met on this journey. Thanks for your support. I appreciate you!

Connect with Elle!

Subscribe to my Newsletter
New Releases, Upcoming projects, and Freebies!

On Facebook,
Join my cocktail lounge for exclusive updates, drink recipes,
and lots of fun!
bit.ly/EllesCocktailLounge

Visit my website: www.ellewright.com

Email me at info@ellewright.com

facebook.com/ellewrightauthor

twitter.com/LWrightAuthor

instagram.com/lwrightauthor

amazon.com/Elle-Wright/e/B00VMEWB78

Also by Elle Wright

CONTEMPORARY ROMANCE

Edge of Scandal Series

The Forbidden Man

His All Night

Her Kind of Man

All He Wants for Christmas

Once Upon a Series

Beyond Forever (Once Upon a Bridesmaid)

Beyond Ever After (Once Upon a Baby)

Finding Cooper (Once Upon a Funeral)

Jacksons of Ann Arbor

It's Always Been You

Wherever You Are

Because Of You

All For You

Wellspring Series

Touched By You

Enticed By You

Pleasured By You

Pure Talent Series

The Way You Tempt Me

The Way You Hold Me

The Way You Love Me

Distinguished Gentlemen Series

The Closing Bid

Women of Park Manor

Her Little Secret

Carnivale Chronicles

Irresistible Temptation

New Year Bae-Solutions

One More Drink

Young In Love Series

It's Not Me, It's You

It's Not Love, It's Business

HISTORICAL ROMANCE

DECADES: A Journey of African American Romance
Made To Hold You (The 80s)

SUSPENSE/THRILLER

Basement Level 5: Never Scared

About the Author

There was never a time when Elle Wright wasn't about to start a book, wasn't already deep in a book—or had just finished one. She grew up believing in the importance of reading, and became a lover of all things romance when her mother gave her her first romance novel. She lives in Michigan.

Connect with Elle!
www.ellewright.com
info@ellewright.com